TEN NIGHTS IN A BAR-ROOM,

AND

WHAT I SAW THERE.

BY

T. S. ARTHUR,

AUTHOR OF "THE BAR-ROOMS AT BRANTLEY," "ORANGE BLOSSOMS,"
ETC., ETC., ETC.

JOHN C. WINSTON CO.,
Chicago,   PHILADELPHIA,   Toronto.

CONTENTS.

vi CONTENTS.

TEN NIGHTS IN A BAR-ROOM.

NIGHT THE FIRST.

THE "SICKLE AND SHEAF."

TEN years ago, business required me to pass a day in Cedarville. It was late in the afternoon when the stage set me down at the "Sickle and Sheaf," a new tavern, just opened by a new landlord, in a new house, built with the special end of providing "accommodations for man and beast." As I stepped from the dusty old vehicle in which I had been jolted along a rough road for some thirty miles, feeling tired and hungry, the good-natured face of Simon Slade, the landlord, beaming as it did with a hearty welcome, was really a pleasant sight to see, and the grasp of his hand was like that of a true friend.

I felt, as I entered the new and neatly furnished sitting-room adjoining the bar, that I had indeed found a comfortable resting-place after my wearisome journey.

"All as nice as a new pin," said I, approvingly, as I glanced around the room, up to the ceiling—white as the driven snow—and over the handsomely carpeted floor. "Haven't seen any thing so inviting as this. How long have you been open?"

"Only a few months," answered the gratified landlord. "But we are not yet in good going order. It takes time, you know, to bring every thing into the right shape. Have you dined yet?"

"No. Every thing looked so dirty at the stage-house, where we stopped to get dinner, that I couldn't venture upon the experiment of eating. How long before your supper will be ready?"

"In an hour," replied the landlord.

"That will do. Let me have a nice piece of tender steak, and the loss of dinner will soon be forgotten."

"You shall have that, cooked fit for an alderman," said the landlord. "I call my wife the best cook in Cedarville."

As he spoke, a neatly dressed girl, about sixteen years of age, with rather an attractive countenance, passed through the room.

"My daughter," said the landlord, as she vanished through the door. There was a sparkle of pride in the father's eyes, and a certain tenderness in the tones of his voice, as he said "My daughter" that told me she was very dear to him.

"You are a happy man to have so fair a child," said I, speaking more in compliment than with a careful choice of words.

"I am a happy man," was the landlord's smiling answer; his fair, round face, unwrinkled by a line of care or trouble, beaming with self-satisfaction. "I have always been a happy man, and always expect to be. Simon Slade takes the world as it comes, and takes it easy. My son, sir," he added, as a boy, in his twelfth year, came in. "Speak to the gentleman."

The boy lifted to mine a pair of deep blue eyes, from which innocence beamed, as he offered me his hand, and said, respectfully— "How do you do, sir?" I could not but remark the girl-like beauty of his face, in which the hardier firmness of the boy's character was already visible.

"What is your name?" I asked.

"Frank, sir."

"Frank is his name," said the landlord—"we called him after his uncle. Frank and Flora— the names sound pleasant to our ears. But, you know, parents are apt to be a little partial and over fond."

"Better that extreme than its opposite," I remarked.

"Just what I always say. Frank, my son," —the landlord spoke to the boy—"there's some one in the bar. You can wait on him as well as I can."

The lad glided from the room, in ready obedience.

"A handy boy that, sir; a very handy boy. Almost as good in the bar as a man. He mixes a toddy or a punch just as well as I can."

"But," I suggested, "are you not a little afraid of placing one so young in the way of temptation."

"Temptation!" The open brows of Simon Slade contracted a little. "No, sir!" he replied, emphatically. "The till is safer under his care than it would be in that of one man in ten. The boy comes, sir, of honest parents. Simon Slade never wronged anybody out of a farthing."

"Oh," said I, quickly, "you altogether misapprehend me. I had no reference to the till, but to the bottle."

The landlord's brows were instantly unbent, and a broad smile circled over his good-humored face.

"Is that all? Nothing to fear, I can assure you. Frank has no taste for liquor, and might pour it out for months without a drop finding its way to his lips. Nothing to apprehend there, sir—nothing."

I saw that further suggestions of danger would be useless, and so remained silent. The arrival of a traveler called away the landlord, and I was left alone for observation and reflection. The bar adjoined the neat sitting-room, and I could see, through the open door, the customer upon whom the lad was attending. He was a well-dressed young man—or rather boy, for he did not appear to be over nineteen years of age—with a fine, intelligent face, that was already slightly marred by sensual indulgence. He raised the glass to his lips, with a quick, almost eager motion, and drained it at a single draught.

"Just right," said he, tossing a sixpence to the young bar-tender. "You are first-rate at a brandy-toddy. Never drank a better in my life."

The lad's smiling face told that he was gratified by the compliment. To me the sight

was painful, for I saw that this youthful tippler was on dangerous ground.

"Who is that young man in the bar?" I
asked, a few minutes afterward, on being re-
joined by the landlord.

Simon Slade stepped to the door and looked
into the bar for a moment.

Two or three men were there by this time;
but he was at no loss in answering my question.

"Oh, that's a son of Judge Hammond, who
lives in the large brick house just as you enter
the village. Willy Hammond, as everybody
familiarly calls him, is about the finest young
man in our neighborhood. There is nothing
proud or put-on about him—nothing—even if
his father is a judge, and rich into the bargain.
Every one, gentle or simple, likes Willy Hammond. And then he is such good company.
Always so cheerful, and always with a pleasant
story on his tongue. And he's so high-spirited
withal, and so honorable. Willy Hammond

would lose his right hand rather than be guilty
of a mean action."

"Landlord!" The voice came loud from the
road in front of the house, and Simon Slade
again left me to answer the demands of some
new-comer. I went into the bar-room, in order
to take a closer observation of Willy Hammond, in whom an interest, not unmingled with
concern, had already been awakened in my
mind. I found him engaged in a pleasant conversation with a plain-looking farmer, whose
homely, terse, common sense was quite as con-
spicuous as his fine play of words and lively
fancy. The farmer was a substantial conserva-
tive, and young Hammond a warm admirer of
new ideas and the quicker adaptation of means
to ends. I soon saw that his mental powers
were developed beyond his years, while his
personal qualities were strongly attractive. I
understood better, after being a silent listener
and observer for ten minutes, why the landlord had spoken of him so warmly.

"Take a brandy-toddy, Mr. H——?" said Hammond, after the discussion closed, good humoredly. "Frank, our junior bar-keeper here, beats his father, in that line."

"I don't care if I do," returned the farmer; and the two passed up to the bar.

"Now, Frank, my boy, don't belie my praises," said the young man; "do your hand-somest."

"Two brandy-toddies, did you say?" Frank made the inquiry with quite a professional air.

"Just what I did say; and let them be equal to Jove's nectar."

Pleased at this familiarity, the boy went briskly to his work of mixing the tempting compound, while Hammond looked on with an approving smile.

"There," said the latter, as Frank passed the glasses across the counter, "if you don't call that first-rate, you're no judge." And he handed one of them to the farmer, who tasted the agreeable draught, and praised its flavor. As before, I noticed that Hammond drank eagerly, like one athirst—emptying his glass without once taking it from his lips.

Soon after the bar-room was empty; and then I walked around the premises, in company with the landlord, and listened to his praise of every thing and his plans and purposes for the future. The house, yard, garden, and out-buildings were in the most perfect order; presenting, in the whole, a model of a village tavern.

"Whatever I do, sir," said the talkative Simon Slade, "I like to do well. I wasn't just raised to tavern-keeping, you must know; but I'm one who can turn his hand to almost any thing."

"What was your business?" I inquired.

"I'm a miller, sir, by trade," he answered— "and a better miller, though I say it myself, is not to be found in Bolton county. I've followed milling these twenty years, and made some little money. But I got tired of hard work, and determined to lead an easier life.

So I sold my mill, and built this house with the money. I always thought I'd like tavern-keeping. It's an easy life; and, if rightly seen after, one in which a man is sure to make money."

"You were still doing a fair business with your mill?"

"Oh, yes. Whatever I do, I do right. Last year, I put by a thousand dollars above all expenses, which is not bad, I can assure you, for a mere grist mill. If the present owner comes out even, he'll do well!"

"How is that?"

"Oh, he's no miller. Give him the best wheat that is grown, and he'll ruin it in grinding. He takes the life out of every grain. I don't believe he'll keep half the custom that I transferred with the mill."

"A thousand dollars, clear profit, in so useful a business, ought to have satisfied you," said I.

"There you and I differ," answered the landlord. "Every man desires to make as much money as possible, and with the least labor. I hope to make two or three thousand dollars a year, over and above all expenses, at tavern-keeping. My bar alone ought to yield me that sum. A man with a wife and children very naturally tries to do as well by them as possible."

"Very true; but," I ventured to suggest, "will this be doing as well by them as if you had kept on at the mill?"

"Two or three thousand dollars a year against one thousand! Where are your figures, man?"

"There may be something beyond the money to take into the account," said I.

"What?" inquired Slade, with a kind of half credulity.

"Consider the different influences of the two callings in life—that of a miller and a tavern-keeper."

"Well! say on."

"Will your children be as safe from temptation here as in their former home?"

"Just as safe," was the unhesitating answer. "Why not?"

I was about to speak of the alluring glass in the case of Frank, but remembering that I had already expressed a fear in that direction, felt that to do so again would be useless, and so kept silent.

"A tavern-keeper," said Slade, "is just as respectable as a miller—in fact, the very people who used to call me 'Simon' or 'Neighbor Dustycoat,' now say 'Landlord,' or Mr. Slade, and treat me in every way more as if I were an equal than ever they did before."

"The change," said I, "may be due to the fact of your giving evidence of possessing some means. Men are very apt to be courteous to those who have property. The building of the tavern has, without doubt, contributed to the new estimation in which you are held."

"That isn't all," replied the landlord. "It is because I am keeping a good tavern, and thus materially advancing the interests of Cedar-ville, that some of our best people look at me with different eyes."

2

"Advancing the interests of Cedarville! In what way?" I did not apprehend his meaning.

"A good tavern always draws people to a place, while a miserable old tumble-down of an affair, badly kept, such as we have had for years, as surely repels them. You can generally tell something about the condition of a town by looking at its taverns. If they are well kept, and doing a good business, you will hardly be wrong in the conclusion that the place is thriving. Why, already, since I built and opened the 'Sickle and Sheaf,' property has advanced over twenty per cent. along the whole street, and not less than five new houses have been commenced."

"Other causes, besides the simple opening of a new tavern, may have contributed to this result," said I.

"None of which I am aware. I was talking with Judge Hammond only yesterday—he owns a great deal of ground on the street—and he did not hesitate to say, that the building and opening of a good tavern here had increased the value of his property at least five thousand dollars. He said, moreover, that he thought the people of Cedarville ought to present me with a silver pitcher; and that, for one, he would contribute ten dollars for the purpose."

The ringing of the supper bell interrupted further conversation; and with the best of appetites, I took my way to the room, where a plentiful meal was spread. As I entered, I met the wife of Simon Slade, just passing out, after seeing that every thing was in order. I had not observed her before; and now could not help remarking that she had a flushed, excited countenance, as if she had been over a hot fire, and was both worried and fatigued. And there was, moreover, a peculiar expression of the mouth, never observed in one whose mind is entirely at ease—an expression that once seen is never forgotten. The face stamped itself, instantly, on my memory; and I can even now recall it with almost the original distinctness. How strongly it contrasted with that of her smiling, self-satisfied husband, who took his place at the head of his table with an air of conscious importance. I was too hungry to talk much, and so found greater enjoyment in eating than in conversation. The landlord had a more chatty guest by his side, and I left them to entertain each other, while I did ample justice to the excellent food with which the table was liberally provided.

After supper I went to the sitting-room, and remained there until the lamps were lighted. A newspaper occupied my time for perhaps half an hour; then the buzz of voices from the adjoining bar-room, which had been increasing for some time, attracted my attention, and I went in there to see and hear what was passing. The first person upon whom my eyes rested was young Hammond, who sat talking with a man older than himself by several years. At a glance, I saw that this man could only associate himself with Willy Hammond as a tempter. Unscrupulous selfishness was written all over his sinister countenance; and I wondered that it did not strike every one, as it did me, with instant repulsion. There could not be, I felt certain, any common ground of association, for two such persons, but the dead level of a village bar-room. I afterward learned, during the evening, that this man's name was Harvey Green, and that he was an occasional visitor at Cedarville, remaining a few days, or a few weeks at a time, as appeared to suit his fancy, and having no ostensible business or special acquaintance with anybody in the village.

"There is one thing about him," remarked Simon Slade, in answering some question that I put in reference to the man, "that I don't object to; he has plenty of money, and is not at all niggardly in spending it. He used to come here, so he told me, about once in five or six months; but his stay at the miserably kept tavern, the only one then in Cedarville, was so uncomfortable, that he had pretty well made up his mind never to visit us again. Now, however, he has engaged one of my best rooms, for which he pays me by the year, and I am to charge him full board for the time he occupies it. He says that there is something about Cedarville that always attracts him; and that his health is better while here than it is anywhere, except South during the winter season. He'll not leave less than two or three hundred dollars a year in our village—there is one item, for you, of advantage to a place in having a good tavern."

"What is his business?" I asked. "Is he engaged in any trading operations?"

The landlord shrugged his shoulders, and looked slightly mysterious, as he answered:

"I never inquire about the business of a guest. My calling is to entertain strangers. If they are pleased with my house, and pay my bills on presentation, I have no right to seek further. As a miller, I never asked a customer whether he raised, bought, or stole his wheat. It was my business to grind it, and I took care to do it well. Beyond that, it was all his own affair. And so it will be in my new calling. I shall mind my own business and keep my own place."

Besides young Hammond and this Harvey Green, there were in the bar-room, when I entered, four others besides the landlord. Among these was a Judge Lyman—so he was addressed—a man between forty and fifty years of age, who had a few weeks before received the Democratic nomination for member of Congress. He was very talkative and very affable, and soon formed a kind of centre of attraction to the bar-room circle. Among other topics of conversation that came up was the new tavern, introduced by the landlord, in whose mind it was, very naturally, the uppermost thought.

"The only wonder to me is," said Judge Lyman, "that nobody had wit enough to see the advantage of a good tavern in Cedarville

ten years ago, or enterprise enough to start
one. I give our friend Slade the credit of
being a shrewd, far-seeing man; and, mark my
word for it, in ten years from to-day he will be
the richest man in the county."

"Nonsense—Ho! ho!" Simon Slade laughed
outright. "The richest man! You forget
Judge Hammond."

"No, not even Judge Hammond, with all
deference for our clever friend Willy," and
Judge Lyman smiled pleasantly on the young
man.

"If he gets richer, somebody will be poorer!" The individual who uttered these words
had not spoken before, and I turned to look at
him more closely. A glance showed him to
be one of a class seen in all bar-rooms; a poor,
broken-down inebriate, with the inward power
of resistance gone—conscious of having no
man's respect, and giving respect to none.
There was a shrewd twinkle in his eyes, as he
fixed them on Slade, that gave added force to

the peculiar tone in which his brief but telling sentence was uttered. I noticed a slight contraction on the landlord's ample forehead, the first evidence I had yet seen of ruffled feelings. The remark, thrown in so untimely (or timely, some will say), and with a kind of prophetic malice, produced a temporary pause in the conversation. No one answered or questioned the intruder, who, I could perceive, silently enjoyed the effect of his words. But soon the obstructed current ran on again.

"If our excellent friend, Mr. Slade," said Harvey Green, "is not the richest man in Cedarville at the end of ten years, he will at least enjoy the satisfaction of having made his town richer."

"A true word that," replied Judge Lyman— "as true a word as ever was spoken. What a dead-and-alive place this has been until within the last few months. All vigorous growth had stopped, and we were actually going to seed."

"And the graveyard too," muttered the indi-

vidual who had before disturbed the self-satisfied harmony of the company, remarking upon
the closing sentence of Harvey Green. "Come,
landlord," he added, as he strode across to the
bar, speaking in a changed, reckless sort of a
way, "fix me up a good hot whisky-punch, and
do it right; and there's another sixpence toward
the fortune you are bound to make. It's the
last one left—not a copper more in my pockets," and he turned them inside-out, with a
half-solemn, half-ludicrous air. "I send it to
keep company in your till with four others
that have found their way into that snug place
since morning, and which will be lonesome
without their little friend."

I looked at Simon Slade; his eyes rested on
mine for a moment or two, and then sunk beneath my earnest gaze. I saw that his countenance flushed, and that his motions were
slightly confused. The incident, it was plain,
did not awaken agreeable thoughts. Once I
saw his hand move toward the sixpence that lay

upon the counter; but whether to push it back or draw it toward the till, I could not determine. The whisky-punch was in due time ready, and with it the man retired to a table across the room, and sat down to enjoy the tempting beverage. As he did so, the landlord quietly swept the poor unfortunate's last sixpence into his drawer. The influence of this strong potation was to render the man a little more talkative. To the free conversation passing around him he lent an attentive ear, dropping in a word, now and then, that always told upon the company like a well-directed blow. At last, Slade lost all patience with him, and said, a little fretfully:

"Look here, Joe Morgan, if you will be ill-natured, pray go somewhere else, and not interrupt good feeling among gentlemen."

"Got my last sixpence," retorted Joe, turning his pockets inside-out again. "No more use for me here to-night. That's the way of the world. How apt a scholar is our good

friend Dustycoat, in this new school! Well,
he was a good miller—no one ever disputed
that—and it's plain to see that he is going to
make a good landlord. I thought his heart
was a little too soft; but the indurating process
has begun, and, in less than ten years, if it
isn't as hard as one of his old millstones, Joe
Morgan is no prophet. Oh, you needn't knit
your brows so, friend Simon, we're old
friends; and friends are privileged to speak
plain."

"I wish you'd go home. You're not yourself, to-night," said the landlord, a little coax-
ingly, for he saw that nothing was to be gained
by quarreling with Morgan. "Maybe my heart
is growing harder," he added, with affected
good-humor; "and it is time, perhaps. One of
my weaknesses, I have heard even you say, was
being too woman-hearted."

"No danger of that now," retorted Joe Morgan. "I've known a good many landlords in
my time, but can't remember one that was

troubled with the disease that once afflicted you."

Just at this moment the outer door was pushed open with a slow, hesitating motion; then a little pale face peered in, and a pair of soft blue eyes went searching about the room. Conversation was instantly hushed, and every face, excited with interest, turned toward the child, who had now stepped through the door. She was not over ten years of age; but it moved the heart to look upon the saddened expression of her young countenance, and the forced bravery therein, that scarcely overcame the native timidity so touchingly visible.

"Father!" I have never heard this word spoken in a voice that sent such a thrill along every nerve. It was full of sorrowful love— full of a tender concern that had its origin too deep for the heart of a child. As she spoke, the little one sprang across the room, and laying her hands upon the arm of Joe Morgan, lifted her eyes, that were ready to gush over with tears, to his face.

"Come, father! won't you come home?" I hear that low, pleading voice even now, and my heart gives a quicker throb. Poor child! Darkly shadowed was the sky that bent gloomily over thy young life.

Morgan arose, and suffered the child to lead him from the room. He seemed passive in her hands. I noticed that he thrust his fingers nervously into his pocket, and that a troubled look went over his face as they were withdrawn. His last sixpence was in the till of Simon Slade!

The first man who spoke was Harvey Green, and this not for a minute after the father and his child had vanished through the door.

"If I was in your place, landlord "—his voice was cold and unfeeling—"I'd pitch that fellow out of the bar-room the next time he stepped through the door. He's no business here, in the first place; and, in the second, he doesn't

"Come, Father! Won't You Come Home?"

know how to behave himself. There's no telling how much a vagabond like him injures a respectable house."

"I wish he would stay away," said Simon, with a perplexed air.

"I'd *make* him stay away," answered Green.

"That may be easier said than done," remarked Judge Lyman. "Our friend keeps a public-house, and can't just say who shall or shall not come into it."

"But such a fellow has no business here. He's a good-for-nothing sot. If I kept a tavern, I'd refuse to sell him liquor."

"That you might do," said Judge Lyman; "and I presume your hint will not be lost on our friend Slade."

"He will have liquor, so long as he can get a cent to buy it with," remarked one of the company; "and I don't see why our landlord here, who has gone to so much expense to fit up a tavern, shouldn't have the sale of it as well as anybody else. Joe talks a little freely sometimes; but no one can say that he is quarrelsome. You've got to take him as he is, that's all."

"I am one," retorted Harvey Green, with a slightly ruffled manner, "who is never disposed to take people as they are when they choose to render themselves disagreeable. If I was Mr. Slade, as I remarked in the beginning, I'd pitch that fellow into the road the next time he put his foot over my door-step."

"Not if I were present," remarked the other, coolly.

Green was on his feet in a moment; and I saw, from the flash of his eyes, that he was a man of evil passions. Moving a pace or two in the direction of the other, he said sharply:

"What is that, sir?"

The individual against whom his anger was so suddenly aroused was dressed plainly, and had the appearance of a working-man. He was stout and muscular.

"I presume you heard my words. They were

spoken distinctly," he replied, not moving from where he sat, nor seeming to be in the least disturbed. But there was cool defiance in the tones of his voice and in the steady look of his eyes.

"You're an impertinent fellow, and I'm half tempted to chastise you."

Green had scarcely finished the sentence, ere he was lying at full length upon the floor! The other had sprung upon him like a tiger, and with one blow from his heavy fist, struck him down as if he had been a child. For a moment or two, Green lay stunned and bewildered—then, starting up with a savage cry, that sounded more bestial than human, he drew a long knife from a concealed sheath, and attempted to stab his assailant; but the murderous purpose was not accomplished, for the other man, who had superior strength and coolness, saw the design, and with a well-directed blow almost broke the arm of Green, causing the knife to leave his hand and glide far across the room.

3

"I'm half tempted to wring your neck off," exclaimed the man, whose name was Lyon, now much excited; and seizing Green by the throat, he strangled him until his face grew black. "Draw a knife on me, ha! You murdering villain!" And he gripped him tighter.

Judge Lyman and the landlord now interfered, and rescued Green from the hands of his fully aroused antagonist. For some time they stood growling at each other, like two parted dogs struggling to get free, in order to renew the conflict, but gradually cooled off. In a little while Judge Lyman drew Green aside, and the two men left the bar-room together. In the door, as they were retiring, the former slightly nodded to Willy Hammond, who soon followed them, going into the sitting-room; and from thence, as I could perceive, up-stairs, to an apartment above.

"Not after much good," I heard Lyon mutter to himself. "If Judge Hammond don't look a little closer after that boy of his, he'll be sorry for it, that's all."

"Who is this Green?" I asked of Lyon, finding myself alone with him in the bar-room, soon after.

"A blackleg, I take it," was his unhesitating answer.

"Does Judge Lyman suspect his real character?"

"I don't know any thing about that; but I wouldn't be afraid to bet ten dollars, that if you could look in upon them now, you would find cards in their hands."

"What a school, and what teachers for the youth who just went with them!" I could not help remarking.

"Willy Hammond?"

"Yes."

"You may well say that. What can his father be thinking about to leave him exposed to such influences!

"He's one of the few who are in raptures

about this tavern, because its erection has slightly increased the value of his property about here; but if he is not the loser of fifty per cent. for every one gained, before ten years go by, I'm very much in error."

"How so?"

"It will prove, I fear, <u>the open door to ruin for his son.</u>"

"That's bad," said I.

"Bad! It is awful to think of. There is not a finer young man in the country, nor one with better mind and heart, than Willy Hammond. So much the sadder will be his destruction. Ah, sir! <u>this tavern-keeping is a curse to any place.</u>"

"But I thought, just now, that you spoke in favor of letting even the poor drunkard's money go into our landlord's till, in order to encourage his commendable enterprise in opening so good a tavern."

"<u>We all speak with covert irony sometimes,</u>" answered the man, "as I did then. Poor Joe

Morgan! He is an old and early friend of
Simon Slade. They were boys together, and
worked as millers under the same roof for many
years. In fact, Joe's father owned the mill, and
the two learned their trade with him. When
old Morgan died, the mill came into Joe's
hands. It was in rather a worn-out condition,
and Joe went in debt for some pretty thorough
repairs and additions of machinery. By and
by, Simon Slade, who was hired by Joe to run
the mill, received a couple of thousand dollars
at the death of an aunt. This sum enabled him
to buy a share in the mill, which Morgan was
very glad to sell in order to get clear of his
debt. Time passed on, and Joe left his milling
interest almost entirely in the care of Slade,
who, it must be said in his favor, did not
neglect the business. But it somehow happened—I will not say unfairly—that at the
end of ten years, Joe Morgan no longer owned
a share in the mill. The whole property was
in the hands of Slade. People did not much

wonder at this; for while Slade was always to be found at the mill, industrious, active, and attentive to customers, Morgan was rarely seen on the premises. You would oftener find him in the woods, with a gun over his shoulder, or sitting by a trout brook, or lounging at the tavern. And yet everybody liked Joe, for he was companionable, quick-witted, and very kind-hearted. He would say sharp things, sometimes, when people manifested little mean-nesses; but there was so much honey in his gall, that bitterness rarely predominated.

"A year or two before his ownership in the mill ceased, Morgan married one of the sweetest girls in our town—Fanny Ellis, that was her name, and she could have had her pick of the young men. Everybody affected to wonder at her choice; and yet nobody really did wonder, for Joe was an attractive young man, take him as you would, and just the one to win the heart of a girl like Fanny. What if he had been seen, now and then, a little the worse for drink! What if he showed more fondness for pleasure than for business! Fanny did not look into the future with doubt or fear. She believed that her love was strong enough to win him from all evil allurements; and, as for this world's goods, they were matters in which her maiden fancies rarely busied themselves.

"Well. Dark days came for her, poor soul! And yet, in all the darkness of her earthly lot, she has never, it is said, been any thing but a loving, forbearing, self-denying wife to Morgan. And he—fallen as he is, and powerless in the grasp of the monster intemperance—has never, I am sure, hurt her with a cruel word. Had he added these, her heart would, long ere this, have broken. Poor Joe Morgan! Poor Fanny! Oh, what a curse is this drink!"

The man, warming with his theme, had spoken with an eloquence I had not expected from his lips. Slightly overmastered by his feelings, he paused for a moment or two, and then added:

"It was unfortunate for Joe, at least, that Slade sold his mill, and became a tavern-keeper; for Joe had a sure berth, and wages regularly paid. He didn't always stick to his work, but would go off on a spree every now and then; but Slade bore with all this, and worked harder himself to make up for his hand's shortcoming. And no matter what deficiency the little store-room at home might show, Fanny Morgan never found her meal barrel empty without knowing where to get it replenished.

"But, after Slade sold the mill, a sad change took place. The new owner was little disposed to pay wages to a hand who would not give him all his time during working hours; and in less than two weeks from the day he took possession, Morgan was discharged. Since then, he has been working about at one odd job and another, earning scarcely enough to buy the liquor it requires to feed the inordinate thirst that is consuming him. I am not disposed to blame Simon Slade for the wrong-doing of

Morgan; but here is a simple fact in the case—if he had kept on at the useful calling of a miller, he would have saved this man's family from want, suffering, and a lower deep of misery than that into which they have already fallen. I merely state it, and you can draw your own conclusion. It is one of the many facts, on the other side of this tavern question, which it will do no harm to mention. I have noted a good many facts besides, and one is, that before Slade opened the "Sickle and Sheaf," he did all in his power to save his early friend from the curse of intemperance; now he has become his tempter. Heretofore, it was his hand that provided the means for his family to live in some small degree of comfort; now he takes the poor pittance the wretched man earns, and dropping it in his till, forgets the wife and children at home who are hungry for the bread this money should have purchased.

"Joe Morgan, fallen as he is, sir, is no fool His mind sees quickly yet; and he rarely utte a sentiment that is not full of meaning. When he spoke of Slade's heart growing as hard in ten years as one of his old mill-stones, he was not uttering words at random, nor merely indulging in a harsh sentiment, little caring whether it were closely applicable or not. That the indurating process had begun, he, alas! was too sadly conscious."

The landlord had been absent from the room for some time. He left soon after Judge Lyman, Harvey Green, and Willy Hammond withdrew, and I did not see him again during the evening. His son Frank was left to attend at the bar; no very hard task, for not more than half a dozen called in to drink from the time Morgan left until the bar was closed.

While Mr. Lyon was giving me the brief history just recorded, I noticed a little incident that caused a troubled feeling to pervade my mind. After a man, for whom the landlord's son had prepared a fancy drink, had nearly emptied his glass, he sat it down upon the counter and went out. A tablespoonful or two remained in the glass, and I noticed Frank, after smelling at it two or three times, put the glass to his lips and sip the sweetened liquor. The flavor proved agreeable; for, after tasting it, he raised the glass again and drained every drop.

"Frank!" I heard a low voice, in a warning tone, pronounce the name, and glancing toward a door partly open, that led from the inside of the bar to the yard, I saw the face of Mrs. Slade. It had the same troubled expression I had noticed before, but now blended with more of anxiety.

The boy went out at the call of his mother; and when a new customer entered, I noticed that Flora, the daughter, came in to wait upon him. I noticed, too, that while she poured out the liquor, there was a heightened color on her face, in which I fancied that I saw a tinge of shame. It is certain that she was not in the least gracious to the person on whom she was waiting; and that there was little heart in her manner of performing the task.

Ten o'clock found me alone and musing in the bar-room over the occurrences of the evening. Of all the incidents, that of the entrance of Joe Morgan's child kept the most prominent place in my thoughts. The picture of that mournful little face was ever before me; and I seemed all the while to hear the word "Father," uttered so touchingly, and yet with such a world of childish tenderness. And the man, who would have opposed the most stubborn resistance to his fellow-men, had they sought to force him from the room, going passively, almost meekly out, led by that little child—I could not, for a time, turn my thoughts from the image thereof! And then thought bore me to the wretched home, back to which the gentle, loving child had taken her father, and my heart grew faint in me as imagination busied itself with all the misery there.

And Willy Hammond. The little that I had

heard and seen of him greatly interested me in his favor. Ah! upon what dangerous ground was he treading. How many pitfalls awaited his feet—how near they were to the brink of a fearful precipice, down which to fall was certain destruction. How beautiful had been his life-promise! How fair the opening day of his existence! Alas! the clouds were gathering already, and the low rumble of the distant thunder presaged the coming of a fearful tempest. Was there none to warn him of the danger? Alas! all might now come too late, for so few who enter the path in which his steps were treading will hearken to friendly counsel, or heed the solemn warning. Where was he now? This question recurred over and over again. He had left the bar-room with Judge Lyman and Green early in the evening, and had not made his appearance since. Who and what was Green? And Judge Lyman, was he a man of principle? One with whom it was safe to trust a youth like Willy Hammond?

While I mused thus, the bar-room door opened, and a man past the prime of life, with a somewhat florid face, which gave a strong relief to the gray, almost white hair that, suffered to grow freely, was pushed back, and lay in heavy masses on his coat collar, entered with a hasty step. He was almost venerable in appearance; yet there was in his dark, quick eyes the brightness of unquenched loves, the fires of which were kindled at the altars of selfishness and sensuality. This I saw at a glance. There was a look of concern on his face, as he threw his eyes around the bar-room; and he seemed disappointed, I thought, at finding it empty.

"Is Simon Slade here?"

As I answered in the negative, Mrs. Slade entered through the door that opened from the yard, and stood behind the counter.

"Ah, Mrs. Slade! Good-evening, madam!" he said.

"Good-evening, Judge Hammond."

"Is your husband at home?"

"I believe he is," answered Mrs. Slade. "I think he's somewhere about the house."

"Ask him to step here, will you?"

Mrs. Slade went out. Nearly five minutes went by, during which time Judge Hammond paced the floor of the bar-room uneasily. Then the landlord made his appearance. The free, open, manly, self-satisfied expression of his countenance, which I had remarked on alighting from the stage in the afternoon, was gone. I noticed at once the change, for it was striking. He did not look steadily into the face of Judge Hammond, who asked him, in a low voice, if his son had been there during the evening.

"He was here," said Slade.

"When?"

"He came in some time after dark and stayed, maybe, an hour."

"And hasn't been here since?"

"It's nearly two hours since he left the bar-room," replied the landlord.

Judge Hammond seemed perplexed. There was a degree of evasion in Slade's manner that he could hardly help noticing. To me it was all apparent, for I had lively suspicions that made my observation acute.

Judge Hammond crossed his arms behind him and took three or four strides about the floor.

"Was Judge Lyman here to-night?" he then asked.

"He was," answered Slade.

"Did he and Willy go out together?"

The question seemed an unexpected one for the landlord. Slade appeared slightly confused, and did not answer promptly.

"I—I rather think they did," he said, after a brief hesitation.

"Ah, well! Perhaps he is at Judge Lyman's I will call over there."

And Judge Hammond left the bar-room.

"Would you like to retire, sir?" said the landlord, now turning to me, with a forced smile—I saw that it was forced.

"If you please," I answered.

He lit a candle and conducted me to my room, where, overwearied with the day's exertion, I soon fell asleep, and did not awake until the sun was shining brightly into my windows.

I remained at the village a portion of the day, but saw nothing of the parties in whom the incidents of the previous evening had awakened a lively interest. At four o'clock I left in the stage, and did not visit Cedarville again for a year.

4

NIGHT THE SECOND.

THE CHANGES OF A YEAR.

A CORDIAL grasp of the hand and a few words of hearty welcome greeted me as I alighted from the stage at the "Sickle and Sheaf," on my next visit to Cedarville. At the first glance, I saw no change in the countenance, manner, or general bearing of Simon Slade, the landlord. With him, the year seemed to have passed like a pleasant summer day. His face was round, and full, and rosy, and his eyes sparkled with that good-humor which flows from intense self-satisfaction. Every thing about him seemed to say—" All right with myself and the world."

I had scarcely expected this. From what I saw during my last brief sojourn at the "Sickle and Sheaf," the inference was natural, that ele ments had been called into activity, which must produce changes adverse to those pleasant states of mind that threw an almost perpetual sun-shine over the landlord's countenance. How many hundreds of times had I thought of Joe Morgan and Willy Hammond—of Frank, and the temptations to which a bar-room exposed him. The heart of Slade must, indeed, be as hard as one of his old mill-stones, if he could remain an unmoved witness of the corruption and degradation of these.

"My fears have outrun the actual progress of things," said I to myself, with a sense of relief, as I mused alone in the still neatly ar-ranged sitting-room, after the landlord, who sat and chatted for a few minutes, had left me. "There is, I am willing to believe, a basis of good in this man's character, which has led him to remove, as far as possible, the more palpable evils that ever attach themselves to a house of public entertainment. He had but entered on the business last year. There was much to be learned, pondered, and corrected. Experience, I doubt not, has led to many important changes in the manner of conducting the establishment, and especially in what pertains to the bar."

As I thought thus, my eyes glanced through the half-open door, and rested on the face of Simon Slade. He was standing behind his bar —evidently alone in the room—with his head bent in a musing attitude. At first I was in some doubt as to the identity of the singularly changed countenance. Two deep perpendicular seams lay sharply defined on his forehead—the arch of his eyebrows was gone, and from each corner of his compressed lips, lines were seen reaching half-way to the chin. Blending with a slightly troubled expression, was a strongly marked selfishness, evidently brooding over the consummation of its purpose. For some moments I sat gazing on his face, half doubting at times if it were really that of Simon Slade. Suddenly, a gleam flashed over it—an ejaculation was uttered, and one clenched hand brought down, with a sharp stroke, into the open palm of the other. The landlord's mind had reached a conclusion, and was resolved upon action. There were no warm rays in the gleam of light that irradiated his countenance—at least none for my heart, which felt under them an almost icy coldness.

"Just the man I was thinking about," I heard the landlord say, as some one entered the bar, while his whole manner underwent a sudden change.

"The old saying is true," was answered in a voice, the tones of which were familiar to my ears.

"Thinking of the old Harry?" said Slade.

"Yes."

"True, literally, in the present case," I heard the landlord remark, though in a much lower tone; "for, if you are not the devil himself, you can't be farther removed than a second cousin."

A low, gurgling laugh met this little sally.

There was something in it so unlike a human laugh, that it caused my blood to trickle, for a moment, coldly along my veins.

I heard nothing more except the murmur of voices in the bar, for a hand shut the partly opened door that led from the sitting-room.

Whose was that voice? I recalled its tones, and tried to fix in my thought the person to whom it belonged, but was unable to do so. I was not very long in doubt, for on stepping out upon the porch in front of the tavern, the well-remembered face of Harvey Green presented itself. He stood in the bar-room door, and was talking earnestly to Slade, whose back was toward me. I saw that he recognized me, although I had not passed a word with him on the occasion of my former visit; and there was a lighting up of his countenance as if about to speak—but I withdrew my eyes from his face to avoid the unwelcome greeting. When I looked at him again, I saw that he was regarding me with a sinister glance, which was instantly withdrawn. In what broad, black characters was the word TEMPTER written on his face! How was it possible for any one to look thereon, and not read the warning in-scription!

Soon after, he withdrew into the bar-room, and the landlord came and took a seat near me on the porch.

"How is the Sickle and Sheaf coming on?" I inquired.

"First-rate," was the answer—"First-rate."

"As well as you expected?"

"Better."

"Satisfied with your experiment?"

"Perfectly. Couldn't get me back to the rumbling old mill again, if you were to make me a present of it."

"What of the mill?" I asked. "How does the new owner come on?"

"About as I thought it would be."

"Not doing very well?"

"How could it be expected, when he didn't

know enough of the milling business to grind
a bushel of wheat right. He lost half of the
custom I transferred to him in less than three
months. Then he broke his main shaft, and it
took over three weeks to get in a new one.
Half of his remaining customers discovered by
this time, that they could get far better meal
from their grain at Harwood's mill near Lyn
wood, and so did not care to trouble him any
more. The upshot of the whole matter is, he
broke down next, and had to sell the mill at a
heavy loss."

"Who has it now?"

"Judge Hammond is the purchaser."

"He is going to rent it, I suppose?"

"No; I believe he means to turn it into some
kind of a factory--and, I rather think, will con-
nect therewith a distillery. This is a fine grain-
growing country, as you know. If he does set
up a distillery, he'll make a fine thing of it.
Grain has been too low in this section for some
years; this all the farmers have felt, and they

are very much pleased at the idea. It will help them wonderfully. I always thought my mill a great thing for the farmers; but what I did for them was a mere song compared to the advantage of an extensive distillery."

"Judge Hammond is one of your richest men?"

"Yes—the richest in the county. And what is more, he's a shrewd, far-seeing man, and knows how to multiply his riches."

"How is his son Willy coming on?"

"Oh! first-rate."

The landlord's eyes fell under the searching look I bent upon him.

"How old is he now?"

"Just twenty."

"A critical age," I remarked.

"So people say; but I didn't find it so," answered Slade, a little distantly.

"The impulses within and the temptations without, are the measure of its dangers. At his age, you were, no doubt, daily employed at hard work."

"I was, and no mistake."

"Thousands and hundreds of thousands are indebted to useful work, occupying many hours through each day, and leaving them with wearied bodies at night, for their safe passage from yielding youth to firm, resisting manhood. It might not be with you as it is now, had leisure and freedom to go in and out when you pleased been offered at the age of nineteen."

"I can't tell as to that," said the landlord, shrugging his shoulders. "But I don't see that Willy Hammond is in any especial danger. He is a young man with many admirable qualities —is social—liberal—generous almost to a fault —but has good common sense, and wit enough, I take it, to keep out of harm's way."

A man passing the house at the moment, gave Simon Slade an opportunity to break off a conversation that was not, I could see, altogether agreeable. As he left me, I arose and stepped into the bar-room. Frank, the landlord's son, was behind the bar. He had grown considerably in the year—and from a rather delicate, innocent-looking boy, to a stout, bold lad. His face was rounder, and had a gross, sensual expression, that showed itself particularly about the mouth. The man Green was standing beside the bar talking to him, and I noticed that Frank laughed heartily, at some low, half obscene remarks that he was making. In the midst of these, Flora, the sister of Frank, a really beautiful girl, came in to get something from the bar. Green spoke to her familiarly, and Flora answered him with a perceptibly heightening color.

I glanced toward Frank, half expecting to see an indignant flush on his young face. But no —he looked on with a smile! "Ah!" thought I, "have the boy's pure impulses so soon died out in this fatal atmosphere? Can he bear to see those evil eyes—he knows they are evil— rest upon the face of his sister? or to hear those lips, only a moment since polluted with vile words, address her with the familiarity of a friend?"

"Fine girl, that sister of yours, Frank! Fine girl!" said Green, after Flora had withdrawn —speaking of her with about as much respect in his voice as if he were praising a fleet racer or favorite hound.

The boy smiled, with a pleased air.

"I must try and find her a good husband, Frank. I wonder if she wouldn't have me?"

"You'd better ask her," said the boy, laughing.

"I would, if I thought there was any chance for me."

"Nothing like trying. Faint heart never won fair lady," returned Frank, more with the air of a man than a boy. How fast he was growing old!

"A banter, by George!" exclaimed Green, slapping his hands together. "You're a great boy, Frank! a great boy! I shall have to talk to your father about you. Coming on too fast. Have to be put back in your lessons—hey!"

And Green winked at the boy, and shook his finger at him. Frank laughed in a pleased way, as he replied:

"I guess I'll do."

"I guess you will," said Green, as, satisfied with his colloquy, he turned off and left the bar-room.

"Have something to drink, sir?" inquired Frank, addressing me in a bold, free way.

I shook my head.

"Here's a newspaper," he added.

I took the paper and sat down—not to read, but to observe. Two or three men soon came in, and spoke in a very familiar way to Frank, who was presently busy setting out the liquors they had called for. Their conversation, interlarded with much that was profane and vulgar, was of horses, horse-racing, gunning, and the like, to all of which the young bar-keeper lent an attentive ear, putting in a word now and then, and showing an intelligence in such matters quite beyond his age. In the midst

thereof, Mr. Slade made his appearance. His
presence caused a marked change in Frank, who
retired from his place among the men, a step
or two outside of the bar, and did not make a
remark while his father remained. It was plain
from this, that Mr. Slade was not only aware
of Frank's dangerous precocity, but had already
marked his forwardness by rebuke.

So far, all that I had seen and heard impressed me unfavorably, notwithstanding the
declaration of Simon Slade, that every thing
about the "Sickle and Sheaf" was coming on
"first-rate," and that he was "perfectly satisfied" with his experiment. Why, even if the
man had gained, in money, fifty thousand dollars by tavern-keeping in a year, he had lost a
jewel in the innocence of his boy that was beyond all valuation. "Perfectly satisfied?"
Impossible! He was not perfectly satisfied.
How could he be? The look thrown upon
Frank when he entered the bar-room, and saw
him "hale fellow, well met," with three or four

idle, profane, drinking customers, contradicted that assertion.

After supper, I took a seat in the bar-room, to see how life moved on in that place of rendezvous for the surface-population of Cedarville. Interest enough in the characters I had met there a year before remained for me to choose this way of spending the time, instead of visiting at the house of a gentleman who had kindly invited me to pass an evening with his family.

The bar-room custom, I soon found, had largely increased in a year. It now required, for a good part of the time, the active services of both the landlord and his son to meet the calls for liquor. What pained me most, was to see the large number of lads and young men who came in to lounge and drink; and there was scarcely one of them whose face did not show marks of sensuality, or whose language was not marred by obscenity, profanity, or vulgar slang. The subjects of conversation were varied enough, though politics was the most prominent. In regard to politics, I heard nothing in the least instructive; but only abuse of individuals and dogmatism on public measures. They were all exceedingly confident in assertion; but I listened in vain for exposition, or even for demonstrative facts. He who asseverated in the most positive manner, and swore the hardest, carried the day in the petty contests.

I noticed, early in the evening, and at a time when all the inmates of the room were in the best possible humor with themselves, the entrance of an elderly man, on whose face I instantly read a deep concern. It was one of those mild, yet strongly marked faces, that strike you at a glance. The forehead was broad, the eyes large and far back in their sockets, the lips full but firm. You saw evidences of a strong, but well-balanced character. As he came in, I noticed a look of intelligence pass from one to another; and then the eyes of two or three were fixed upon a young man who was seated not far from me, with his back to the entrance, playing at dominoes. He had a glass of ale by his side. The old man searched about the room for some moments, before his glance rested upon the individual I have mentioned. My eyes were full upon his face, as he advanced toward him, yet unseen. Upon it was not a sign of angry excitement, but a most touching sorrow.

"Edward!" he said, as he laid his hand gently on the young man's shoulder. The latter started at the voice, and crimsoned deeply. A few moments he sat irresolute.

"Edward, my son!" It would have been a cold, hard heart indeed that softened not under the melting tenderness of these tones. The call was irresistible, and obedience a necessity. The powers of evil had, yet, too feeble a grasp on the young man's heart to hold him in thrall. Rising with a half-reluctant manner, and with a shamefacedness that it was impossible to cast

5

ceal, he retired as quietly as possible. The notice of only a few in the bar-room was attracted by the incident.

"I can tell you what," I heard the individual, with whom the young man had been playing at dominoes, remark—himself not twenty years of age—"if my old man were to make a fool of himself in this way—sneaking around after me in bar-rooms—he'd get only his trouble for his pains. I'd like to see him try it, though! There'd be a nice time of it, I guess. Wouldn't I creep off with him, as meek as a lamb! Ho! ho!"

"Who is that old gentleman who came in just now?" I inquired of the person who thus commented on the incident which had just occurred.

"Mr. Hargrove is his name."

"And that was his son?"

"Yes; and I'm only sorry he doesn't possess a little more spirit."

"How old is he?"

'About twenty."

"Not of legal age, then?"

"He's old enough to be his own master."

"The law says differently," I suggested.

In answer, the young man cursed the law, snapping his fingers in its imaginary face as he did so.

"At least you will admit," said I, "that Edward Hargrove, in the use of a liberty to go where he pleases, and do what he pleases, exhibits but small discretion."

"I will admit no such thing. What harm is there, I would like to know, in a social little game such as we were playing? There were no stakes—we were not gambling."

I pointed to the half-emptied glass of ale left by young Hargrove.

"Oh! oh!" half sneered, half laughed a man, twice the age of the one I had addressed, who sat near by, listening to our conversation. I looked at him for a moment, and then said:

"The great danger lies there, without doubt.

If it were only a glass of ale and a game of dominoes—but it doesn't stop there, and well the young man's father knows it."

"Perhaps he does," was answered. "I remember him in his younger days; and a pretty high boy he was. He didn't stop at a glass of ale and a game at dominoes; not he! I've seen him as drunk as a lord many a time; and many a time at a horse-race, or cock-fight, betting with the bravest. I was only a boy, though a pretty old boy; but I can tell you, Hargrove was no saint."

"I wonder not, then, that he is anxious for his son," was my remark. "He knows well the lurking dangers in the path he seems inclined to enter."

"I don't see that they have done him much harm. He sowed his wild oats—then got married, and settled down into a good, substantial citizen. A little too religious and pharisaical, I always thought; but upright in his dealings. He had his pleasures in early life, as was befit ting the season of youth—why not let his son taste of the same agreeable fruit? He's wrong, sir—wrong! And I've said as much to Ned. I only wish the boy had showed the right spunk this evening, and told the old man to go home about his business."

"So do I," chimed in the young disciple in this bad school. "It's what I'd say to my old man, in double-quick time, if he was to come hunting after me."

"He knows better than to do that," said the other, in a way that let me deeper into the young man's character.

"Indeed he does. He's tried his hand on me once or twice during the last year, but found it wouldn't do, no how; Tom Peters is out of his leading-strings."

"And can drink his glass with any one, and not be a grain the worse for it."

"Exactly, old boy!" said Peters, slapping his preceptor on the knee. "Exactly! I'm not one of your weak-headed ones. Oh no!"

"Look here, Joe Morgan!"—the half-angry voice of Simon Slade now rung through the bar-room,—"just take yourself off home!"

I had not observed the entrance of this person. He was standing at the bar, with an emptied glass in his hand. A year had made no improvement in his appearance. On the contrary, his clothes were more worn and tattered; his countenance more sadly marred. What he had said to irritate the landlord, I know not; but Slade's face was fiery with passion, and his eyes glared threateningly at the poor besotted one, who showed not the least inclination to obey.

"Off with you, I say! And never show your face here again. I won't have such low vagabonds as you are about my house. If you can't keep decent and stay decent, don't intrude yourself here."

"A rum-seller talk of decency!" retorted Morgan. "Pah! You were a decent man once, and a good miller into the bargain. But

"It's Joe Morgan's Child! He's Killed Her! Good Heavens!"

that time's past and gone. Decency died out when you exchanged the pick and facing-hammer for the glass and muddler. Decency! Pah! How you talk! As if it were any more decent to sell rum than to drink it."

There was so much of biting contempt in the tones, as well as the words of the half-intoxicated man, that Slade, who had himself been drinking rather more freely than usual, was angered beyond self-control. Catching up an empty glass from the counter, he hurled it with all his strength at the head of Joe Morgan. The missive just grazed one of his temples, and flew by on its dangerous course. The quick sharp cry of a child startled the air, followed by exclamations of alarm and horror from many voices.

"It's Joe Morgan's child!" "He's killed her!" "Good heavens!" Such were the exclamations that rang through the room. I was among the first to reach the spot where a little girl, just gliding in through the door, had been struck on the forehead by the glass, which had cut a deep gash, and stunned her into insensibility. The blood flowed instantly from the wound, and covered her face, which presented a shocking appearance. As I lifted her from the floor, upon which she had fallen, Morgan, into whose very soul the piercing cry of his child had penetrated, stood by my side, and grappled his arms around her insensible form, uttering as he did so heart-touching moans and lamentations.

"What's the matter? Oh, what's the matter?" It was a woman's voice, speaking in frightened tones.

"It's nothing! Just go out, will you, Ann?" I heard the landlord say.

But his wife—it was Mrs. Slade—having heard the shrieks of pain and terror uttered by Morgan's child, had come running into the barroom—heeded not his words, but pressed forward into the little group that stood around the bleeding girl.

Little girl dead

"Run for Doctor Green, Frank," she cried in an imperative voice, the moment her eyes rested on the little one's bloody face.

Frank came around from behind the bar, in obedience to the word; but his father gave a partial countermand, and he stood still. Upon observing which, his mother repeated the order, even more emphatically.

"Why don't you jump, you young rascal!" exclaimed Harvey Green. "The child may be dead before the doctor can get here."

Frank hesitated no longer, but disappeared instantly through the door.

"Poor, poor child!" almost sobbed Mrs. Slade, as she lifted the insensible form from my arms. "How did it happen? Who struck her?"

"Who? Curse him! Who but Simon Slade?" answered Joe Morgan, through his clenched teeth.

The look of anguish, mingled with bitter reproach, instantly thrown upon the landlord by his wife, can hardly be forgotten by any who saw it that night.

"Oh, Simon! Simon! And has it come to this already?" What a world of bitter memories, and sad forebodings of evil, did that little sentence express. "To this already"—Ah! In the downward way, how rapidly the steps do tread—how fast the progress!

"Bring me a basin of water, and a towel, quickly!" she now exclaimed.

The water was brought, and in a little while the face of the child lay pure and white as snow against her bosom. The wound from which the blood had flowed so freely was found on the upper part of the forehead, a little to the side, and extending several inches back, along the top of the head. As soon as the blood stains were wiped away, and the effusion partially stopped, Mrs. Slade carried the still insensible body into the next room, whither the distressed, and now completely sobered father, accompanied her. I went with them, but Slade remained behind.

The arrival of the doctor was soon followed by the restoration of life to the inanimate body. He happened to be at home, and came instantly. He had just taken the last stitch in the wound, which required to be drawn together, and was applying strips of adhesive plaster, when the hurried entrance of some one caused me to look up. What an apparition met my eyes! A woman stood in the door, with a face in which maternal anxiety and terror blended fearfully. Her countenance was like ashes— her eyes straining wildly—her lips apart, while the panting breath almost hissed through them.

"Joe! Joe! What is it? Where is Mary? Is she dead?" were her eager inquiries.

"No, Fanny," answered Joe Morgan, starting up from where he was actually kneeling by the side of the reviving little one, and going quickly to his wife. "She's better now. It's a bad hurt, but the doctor says it's nothing dangerous. Poor, dear child!"

The pale face of the mother grew paler—she

gasped—caught for breath two or three times
—a low shudder ran through her frame—and
then she lay white and pulseless in the arms of
her husband. As the doctor applied restora-
tives, I had opportunity to note more particularly the appearance of Mrs. Morgan. Her
person was very slender, and her face so atten-
uated that it might almost be called shadowy.
Her hair, which was a rich chestnut brown,
with a slight golden lustre, had fallen from her
comb, and now lay all over her neck and bosom
in beautiful luxuriance. Back from her full
temples it had been smoothed away by the
hand of Morgan, that all the while moved over
her brow and temples with a caressing motion
that I saw was unconscious, and which revealed
the tenderness of feeling with which, debased
as he was, he regarded the wife of his youth,
and the long suffering companion of his later
and evil days. Her dress was plain and coarse,
but clean and well fitting; and about her whole
person was an air of neatness and taste. She

could not now be called beautiful; yet in her marred features—marred by suffering and grief —were many lineaments of beauty; and much that told of a pure, true woman's heart beating in her bosom. Life came slowly back to the stilled heart, and it was nearly half an hour before the circle of motion was fully restored.

Then, the twain, with their child, tenderly borne in the arms of her father, went sadly homeward, leaving more than one heart heavier for their visit.

I saw more of the landlord's wife on this occasion than before. She had acted with a promptness and humanity that impressed me very favorably. It was plain, from her exclamations on learning that her husband's hand inflicted the blow that came so near destroying the child's life, that her faith for good in the tavern-keeping experiment had never been strong. I had already inferred as much. Her face, the few times I had seen her, wore a troubled look; and I could never forget its expression, nor her anxious, warning voice, when she discovered Frank sipping the dregs from a glass in the bar-room.

It is rarely, I believe, that wives consent freely to the opening of taverns by their husbands; and the determination on the part of the latter to do so, is not unfrequently attended with a breach of confidence and good feeling never afterward fully healed. Men look close to the money result; women to the moral consequences. I doubt if there be one dram-seller in ten, between whom and his wife there exists a good understanding—to say nothing of genuine affection. And, in the exceptional cases, it will generally be found that the wife is as mercenary, or careless of the public good, as her husband. I have known some women to set up grog-shops; but they were women of bad principles and worse hearts. I remember one case, where a woman, with a sober, church-going husband, opened a dram-shop. The husband opposed, remonstrated, begged, threatened—but all to no purpose. The wife, by working for the clothing stores, had earned and saved about three hundred dollars. The love of money, in the slow process of accumulation, had been awakened; and, in ministering to the depraved appetites of men who loved drink and neglected their families, she saw a quicker mode of acquiring the gold she coveted. And so the dram-shop was opened. And what was the result? The husband quit going to church. He had no heart for that; for, even on the Sabbath day, the fiery stream was stayed not in his house. Next he began to tipple. Soon, alas! the subtle poison so pervaded his system that morbid desire came; and then he moved along quick-footed in the way to ruin. In less than three years, I think, from the time the grog-shop was opened by his wife, he was in a drunkard's grave. A year or two more, and the pit that was digged for others by the hands of the wife, she fell into herself. Ever breathing an atmosphere poisoned by the fumes of liquor, the

love of tasting it was gradually formed, and
she too, in the end, became a slave to the
Demon of Drink. She died, at last, poor as a
beggar in the street. Ah! this liquor-selling
is the way to ruin; and they who open the
gates, as well as those who enter the downward
path, alike go to destruction. But this is di-
gressing.

After Joe Morgan and his wife left the
"Sickle and Sheaf," with that gentle child,
who, as I afterward learned, had not, for a year
or more, laid her little head to sleep until her
father returned home—and who, if he stayed
out beyond a certain hour, would go for him,
and lead him back, a very angel of love and
patience—I re-entered the bar-room, to see how
life was passing there. Not one of all I had
left in the room remained. The incident which
had occurred was of so painful a nature, that
no further unalloyed pleasure was to be had
there during the evening, and so each had retired. In his little kingdom the landlord sat

alone, his head resting on his hand, and his face shaded from the light. The whole aspect of the man was that of one in self-humiliation. As I entered he raised his head, and turned his face toward me. Its expression was painful.

"Rather an unfortunate affair," said he. "I'm angry with myself, and sorry for the poor child. But she'd no business here. As for Joe Morgan, it would take a saint to bear his tongue when once set a-going by liquor. I wish he'd stay away from the house. Nobody wants his company. Oh, dear!"

The ejaculation, or rather groan, that closed the sentence showed how little Slade was satisfied with himself, notwithstanding this feeble effort at self-justification.

"His thirst for liquor draws him hither," I remarked. "The attraction of your bar to his appetite is like that of the magnet to the needle. He cannot stay away."

"He *must* stay away!" exclaimed the land-

6

lord, with some vehemence of tone, striking his fist upon the table by which he sat. "He *must* stay away! There is scarcely an evening that he does not ruffle my temper, and mar good feelings in all the company. Just see what he provoked me to do this evening. I might have killed the child. It makes my blood run cold to think of it! Yes, sir—he must stay away. If no better can be done, I'll hire a man to stand at the door and keep him out."

"He never troubled you at the mill," said I. "No man was required at the mill door?"

"No!" And the landlord gave emphasis to the word by an oath, ejaculated with a heartiness that almost startled me. I had not heard him swear before. "No; the great trouble was to get him and keep him there, the good-for-nothing, idle fellow!"

"I'm afraid," I ventured to suggest, "that things don't go on quite so smoothly here as they did at the mill. Your customers are of a different class."

"I don't know about that; why not?" He did not just relish my remark.

"Between quiet, thrifty, substantial farmers, and drinking bar-room loungers, are many degrees of comparison."

"Excuse me, sir!" Simon Slade elevated his person. "The men who visit my bar-room, as a general thing, are quite as respectable, moral, and substantial as any who came to the mill—and I believe more so. The first people in the place, sir, are to be found here. Judge Lyman and Judge Hammond; Lawyer Wilks and Doctor Maynard; Mr. Grand and Mr. Lee; and dozens of others—all our first people. No, sir; you mustn't judge all by vagabonds like Joe Morgan."

There was a testy spirit manifested that I did not care to provoke. I could have met his assertion with facts and inferences of a character to startle any one occupying his

position, who was in a calm, reflective state;
but to argue with him then would have been
worse than idle; and so I let him talk on until
the excitement occasioned by my words died
out for want of new fuel.

NIGHT THE THIRD.

JOE MORGAN'S CHILD.

" I DON'T see any thing of your very particu-lar friend, Joe Morgan, this evening," said Harvey Green, leaning on the bar and speak-ing to Slade. It was the night succeeding that on which the painful and exciting scene with the child had occurred.

"No," was answered—and to the word was added a profane imprecation. "No; and if he'll just keep away from here, he may go to —— on a hard-trotting horse and a porcupine saddle as fast as he pleases. He's tried my pa-tience beyond endurance, and my mind is made up, that he gets no more drams at this bar. I've borne his vile tongue and seen my com-pany annoyed by him just as long as I mean to stand it. Last night decided me. Suppose I'd killed that child?"

"You'd have had trouble then, and no mistake."

"Wouldn't I? Blast her little picture! What business has she creeping in here every night?"

"She must have a nice kind of a mother," remarked Green, with a cold sneer.

"I don't know what she is now," said Slade, a slight touch of feeling in his voice—"heart-broken, I suppose. I couldn't look at her last night; it made me sick. But there was a time when Fanny Morgan was the loveliest and best woman in Cedarville. I'll say that for her. Oh, dear! What a life her miserable husband has caused her to lead."

"Better that he were dead and out of the way."

"Better a thousand times," answered Slade. "If he'd only fall down some night and break his neck, it would be a blessing to his family."

"And to you in particular," laughed Green.

"You may be sure it wouldn't cost me a large sum for mourning," was the unfeeling response.

Let us leave the bar-room of the "Sickle and Sheaf," and its cold-hearted inmates, and look in upon the family of Joe Morgan, and see how it is in the home of the poor inebriate. We will pass by a quick transition.

"Joe!" The thin white hand of Mrs. Morgan clasps the arm of her husband, who has arisen up suddenly, and now stands by the partly opened door. "Don't go out to-night, Joe. Please, don't go out."

"Father!" A feeble voice calls from the corner of an old settee, where little Mary lies with her head bandaged.

"Well, I won't then!" is replied—not angrily, nor even fretfully.—but in a kind voice.

"Come and sit by me, father." How tenderly, yet how full of concern is that low, sweet voice. "Come, won't you?"

"Yes, dear."

"Now hold my hand, father."

Joe takes the hand of little Mary, that instantly lightens upon his.

"You won't go away and leave me to-night, will you, father? Say you won't."

"How very hot your hand is, dear. Does your head ache?"

"A little; but it will soon feel better."

Up into the swollen and disfigured face of the fallen father, the large, earnest blue eyes of the child are raised. She does not see the marred lineaments; but only the beloved countenance of her parent.

"Dear father!"

"What, love?"

"I wish you'd promise me something."

"What, dear?"

"Will you promise?"

"I can't say until I hear your request. If I can promise, I will."

"Oh! you can promise—you can, father!"

How the large blue eyes dance and sparkle!

"What is it, love?"

"That you'll never go into Simon Slade's bar any more."

The child raises herself, evidently with a painful effort; and leans nearer to her father.

Joe shakes his head, and poor Mary drops back upon her pillow with a sigh. Her lids fall, and the long lashes lie strongly relieved on her colorless cheeks.

"I won't go there to-night, dear. So let your heart be at rest."

Mary's lids unclose, and two round drops, released from their clasp, glide slowly over her face.

"Thank you, father—thank you. Mother will be so glad."

The eyes closed again; and the father moved uneasily. His heart is touched. There is a struggle within him. It is on his lips to say that he will never drink at the "Sickle and Sheaf" again; but resolution just lacks the force of utterance.

"Father!"

"Well, dear?"

"I don't think I'll be well enough to go out in two or three days. You know the doctor said that I would have to keep very still, for I had a great deal of fever."

"Yes, poor child."

"Now, won't you promise me one thing?"

"What is it, dear?"

"Not to go out in the evening until I get well."

Joe Morgan hesitated.

"Just promise me that, father. It won't be long; I shall be up again in a little while."

How well the father knows what is in the heart of his child. Her fears are all for him. Who is to go after her poor father, and lead him home when the darkness of inebriety is on his spirit, and external perception so dulled that not skill enough remains to shun the harm that lies in his path?

"Do promise just that, father, dear."

He cannot resist the pleading voice and look.

"I promise it, Mary; so shut your eyes now and go to sleep. I'm afraid this fever will increase."

"Oh! I'm so glad—so glad!"

Mary does not clasp her hands, nor show strong external signs of pleasure; but how full of a pure, unselfish joy is that low-murmured ejaculation, spoken in the depths of her spirit, as well as syllabled by her tongue!

Mrs. Morgan has been no unconcerned witness of all this; but knowing the child's influence over her father, she has not ventured a word. More was to be gained, she was sure, by silence on her part; and so she has kept silent. Now she comes nearer to them, and says, as she lets a hand rest on the shoulder of her husband:

"You feel better for that promise already; I know you do."

He looks up to her, and smiles faintly. He does feel better, but is hardly willing to acknowledge it.

Soon after Mary is sleeping. It does not escape the observation of Mrs. Morgan that her husband grows restless; for he gets up suddenly, every now and then, and walks quickly across the room, as if in search of something. Then sits down, listlessly—sighs—stretches himself, and says, "Oh, dear!" What shall she do for him? How is the want of his accustomed evening stimulus to be met? She thinks, and questions, and grieves inwardly. Poor Joe Morgan! His wife understands his case, and pities him from her heart. But what can she do? Go out and get him something to drink? "Oh, no! no! no! never!" She answered the thought audibly almost, in the excitement of her feelings. An hour has passed—Joe's restlessness has increased instead of diminishing. What is to be done? Now Mrs. Morgan has left the room. She has resolved upon something, for the case must be met. Ah! here she comes, after an absence of five minutes, bearing in her hand a cup of strong coffee.

" It was kind and thoughtful in you, Fanny,"
says Morgan, as with a gratified look he takes
the cup. But his hand trembles, and he spills
a portion of the contents as he tries to raise it
to his lips. How dreadfully his nerves are
shattered! Unnatural stimulants have been
applied so long, that all true vitality seems
lost.

And now the hand of his wife is holding the
cup to his lips, and he drinks eagerly.

" This is dreadful—dreadful! Where will it
end? What is to be done?"

Fanny suppresses a sob, as she thus gives
vent to her troubled feelings. Twice, already,
has her husband been seized with the drunkard's madness; and, in the nervous prostration
consequent upon even a brief withdrawal of his
usual strong stimulants, she sees the fearful pre-
cursor of another attack of this dreadful and
dangerous malady. In the hope of supplying
the needed tone she has given him strong coffee; and this, for the time, produces the effect

desired. The restlessness is allayed, and a quiet state of body and mind succeeds. It needs but a suggestion to induce him to retire for the night. After being a few minutes in bed, sleep steals over him, and his heavy breathing tells that he is in the world of dreams.

And now there comes a tap at the door.

"Come in," is answered.

The latch is lifted, the door swings open, and a woman enters.

"Mrs. Slade!" The name is uttered in a tone of surprise.

"Fanny, how are you this evening?" Kindly, yet half sadly, the words are said.

"Tolerable, I thank you."

The hands of the two women are clasped, and for a few moments they gaze into each other's face. What a world of tender commiseration is in that of Mrs. Slade!

"How is little Mary to-night?"

"Not so well, I'm afraid. She has a good deal of fever."

"Indeed! Oh, I'm sorry! Poor child! what a dreadful thing it was! Oh! Fanny! you don't know how it has troubled me. I've been in·tending to come around all day to see how she was, but couldn't get off until now."

"It came near killing her," said Mrs. Morgan.

"It's in God's mercy she escaped. The thought of it curdles the very blood in my veins. Poor child! is this her on the settee?"

"Yes."

Mrs. Slade takes a chair, and sitting by the sleeping child, gazes long upon her pale sweet face. Now the lips of Mary part—words are murmured—what is she saying?

"No, no, mother; I can't go to bed yet. Father isn't home. And it's so dark. There's no one to lead him over the bridge. I'm not afraid. Don't—don't cry so, mother—I'm not afraid! Nothing will hurt me."

The child's face flushes. She moans, and throws her arms about uneasily. Hark again.

"I wish Mr. Slade wouldn't look so cross at

me. He never did when I went to the mill.
He doesn't take me on his knee now, and stroke
my hair. Oh, dear! I wish father wouldn't go
there any more. Don't! don't, Mr. Slade. Oh!
oh!"—the ejaculation prolonged into a frightened cry, "My head! my head!"

A few choking sobs are followed by low
moans; and then the child breathes easily
again. But the flush does not leave her cheek;
and when Mrs. Slade, from whose eyes the
tears come forth drop by drop, and roll down
her face, touches it lightly, she finds it hot with
fever.

"Has the doctor seen her to-day, Fanny?"

"No, ma'am."

"He should see her at once. I will go for
him;" and Mrs. Slade starts up and goes
quickly from the room. In a little while she
returns with Doctor Green, who sits down and
looks at the child for some moments with a
sober, thoughtful face. Then he lays his fingers on her pulse and times its beat by his

watch — shakes his head, and looks graver still.

"How long has she had fever?" he asks.

"All day."

"You should have sent for me earlier."

"Oh, doctor! She is not dangerous, I hope?" Mrs. Morgan looks frightened.

"She's a sick child, madam."

"You've promised, father."—The dreamer is speaking again.—"I'm not well enough yet. Oh, don't go, father; don't! There! He's gone! Well, well! I'll try and walk there— I can sit down and rest by the way. Oh, dear! How tired I am! Father! Father!"

The child starts up and looks about her wildly.

"Oh, mother, is it you?" And she sinks back upon her pillow, looking now inquiringly from face to face.

"Father—where is father?" she asks.

"Asleep, dear."

"Oh! Is he? I'm glad."

7

Her eyes close wearily.

"Do you feel any pain, Mary?" inquired the doctor.

' Yes, sir—in my head. It aches and beats so."

The cry of "Father" has reached the ears of Morgan, who is sleeping in the next room, and roused him into consciousness. He knows the doctor's voice. Why is he here at this late hour? "Do you feel any pain, Mary?" The question he hears distinctly, and the faintly uttered reply also. He is sober enough to have all his fears instantly excited. There is nothing in the world that he loves as he loves that child. And so he gets up and dresses himself as quickly as possible; the stimulus of anxiety giving tension to his relaxed nerves.

"Oh, father!" The quick ears of Mary detect his entrance first, and a pleasant smile welcomes him.

"Is she very sick, doctor?" he asks, in a voice full of anxiety.

"She's a sick child, sir; you should have sent for me earlier." The doctor speaks rather sternly, and with a purpose to rebuke.

The reply stirs Morgan, and he seems to cower half-timidly under the words, as if they were blows. Mary has already grasped her father's hand, and holds on to it tightly.

After examining the case a little more closely, the doctor prepares some medicine, and promising to call early in the morning, goes away. Mrs. Slade follows soon after; but, in parting with Mrs. Morgan, leaves something in her hand, which, to the surprise of the latter, proves to be a ten-dollar bill. The tears start to her eyes; and she conceals the money in her bosom—murmuring a fervent "God bless her!"

A simple act of restitution is this on the part of Mrs. Slade, prompted as well by humanity as a sense of justice. With one hand her husband has taken the bread from the family of his old friend, and thus with the other she restores it.

And now Morgan and his wife are alone with their sick child. Higher the fever rises, and partial delirium seizes upon her over-excited brain. She talks for a time almost incessantly. All her trouble is about her father; and she is constantly referring to his promise not to go out in the evening until she gets well. How tenderly and touchingly she appeals to him; now looking up into his face in partial recognition; and now calling anxiously after him, as if he had left her and was going away.

"You'll not forget your promise, will you, father?" she says, speaking so calmly, that he thinks her mind has ceased to wander.

"No, dear; I will not forget it," he answers, smoothing her hair gently with his hand.

"You'll not go out in the evening again, until I get well?"

"No, dear."

"Father!"

"What, love?"

"Stoop down closer; I don't want mother to hear; it will make her feel so bad."

The father bends his ear close to the lips of Mary. How he starts and shudders! What has she said?—only these brief words:

"I shall not get well, father; I'm going to die."

The groans, impossible to repress, that issued through the lips of Joe Morgan, startled the ears of his wife, and she came quickly to the bed-side.

"What is it? What is the matter, Joe?" she inquired, with a look of anxiety.

"Hush, father. Don't tell her. I only said it to you." And Mary put a finger on her lips, and looked mysterious. "There, mother—you go away; you've got trouble enough, any how. Don't tell her, father."

But the words, which came to him like a prophecy, awoke such pangs of fear and re-morse in the heart of Joe Morgan, that it was impossible for him to repress the signs of pain.

For some moments he gazed at his wife—-then
stooping forward, suddenly, he buried his face
in the bed-clothes, and sobbed bitterly.

A suggestion of the truth now flashed through
the mind of Mrs. Morgan, sending a thrill of
pain along every nerve. Ere she had time to
recover herself, the low, sweet voice of Mary
broke upon the hushed air of the room, and
she sung:

> " Jesus can make a dying bed
>   Feel soft as downy pillows are,
> While on His breast I lean my head,
>   And breathe my life out, sweetly, there."

It was impossible for Mrs. Morgan longer to
repress her feelings. As the softly breathed
strain died away, her sobs broke forth, and for
a time she wept violently.

"There," said the child,—"I didn't mean to
tell you. I only told father, because—because
he promised not to go to the tavern any more
until I got well; and I'm not going to get well.
So, you see, mother, he'll never go again—never

—never—never. Oh, dear! how my head pains. Mr. Slade threw it so hard. But it didn't strike father; and I'm so glad. How it would have hurt him—poor father! But he'll never go there any more; and that will be so good, won't it, mother?"

A light broke over her face; but seeing that her mother still wept, she said:

"Don't cry. Maybe I'll be better."

And then her eyes closed heavily, and she slept again.

"Joe," said Mrs. Morgan, after she had in a measure recovered herself—she spoke firmly—"Joe, did you hear what she said?"

Morgan only answered with a groan.

"Her mind wanders; and yet she may have spoken only the truth."

He groaned again.

"If she should die, Joe——"

"Don't; oh, don't talk so, Fanny. She's not going to die. It's only because she's a little light-headed."

"Why is she light-headed, Joe?"

"It's the fever—only the fever, Fanny."

"It was the blow, and the wound on her head, that caused the fever. How do we know the extent of injury on the brain? Doctor Green looked very serious. I'm afraid, husband, that the worst is before us. I've borne and suffered a great deal—only God knows how much—I pray that I may have strength to bear this trial also. Dear child! She is better fitted for heaven than for earth, and it may be that God is about to take her to Himself. She's been a great comfort to me—and to you, Joe, more like a guardian angel than a child."

Mrs. Morgan had tried to speak very firmly; but as sentence followed sentence, her voice lost more and more of its even tone. With the closing words all self-control vanished; and she wept bitterly. What could her feeble erring husband do, but weep with her?

"Joe,"—Mrs. Morgan aroused herself as

quickly as possible, for she had that to say which she feared she might not have the heart to utter—"Joe, if Mary dies, you cannot forget the cause of her death."

"Oh, Fanny! Fanny!"

"Nor the hand that struck the cruel blow."

"Forget it? Never! And if I forgive Simon Slade——"

"Nor the place where the blow was dealt," said Mrs. Morgan, interrupting him.

"Poor—poor child!" moaned the conscience-stricken man.

"Nor your promise, Joe—nor your promise given to our dying child."

"Father! Father! Dear father!" Mary's eyes suddenly unclosed, as she called her father eagerly.

"Here I am, love. What is it?" And Joe Morgan pressed up to the bed-side.

"Oh! it's you, father! I dreamed that you had gone out, and—and—but you won't, will you, dear father?"

"No, love—no."

"Never any more until I get well?"

"I must go out to work, you know, Mary."

"At night, father. That's what I mean. You won't, will you?"

"No, dear, no."

A soft smile trembled over the child's face; her eyelids drooped wearily, and she fell off into slumber again. She seemed not so restless as before—did not moan, nor throw herself about in her sleep.

"She's better, I think," said Morgan, as he bent over her, and listened to her softer breathing.

"It seems so," replied his wife. "And now, Joe, you must go to bed again. I will lie down here with Mary, and be ready to do any thing for her that she may want."

"I don't feel sleepy. I'm sure I couldn't close my eyes. So let me sit up with Mary. You are tired and worn out."

Mrs. Morgan looked earnestly into her husband's face. His eyes were unusually bright, and she noticed a slight nervous restlessness about his lips. She laid one of her hands on his, and perceived a slight tremor.

"You must go to bed," she spoke firmly. "I shall not let you sit up with Mary. So go at once." And she drew him almost by force into the next room.

"It's no use, Fanny. There's not a wink of sleep in my eyes. I shall lie awake anyhow. So do you get a little rest."

Even as he spoke there were nervous twitchings of his arms and shoulders; and as he entered the chamber, impelled by his wife, he stopped suddenly and said:

"What is that?"

"Where?" asked Mrs. Morgan.

"Oh, it's nothing—I see. Only one of my old boots. I thought it a great black cat."

Oh! what a shudder of despair seized upon the heart of the wretched wife. Too well she knew the fearful signs of that terrible madness from which, twice before, he had suffered. She could have looked on calmly and seen him die—but, "Not this—not this! Oh, Father in heaven!" she murmured, with such a heart-sinking that it seemed as if life itself would go out.

"Get into bed, Joe; get into bed as quickly as possible."

Morgan was now passive in the hands of his wife, and obeyed her almost like a child. He had turned down the bed-clothes, and was about getting in, when he started back, with a look of disgust and alarm.

"There's nothing there, Joe. What's the matter with you?"

"I'm sure I don't know, Fanny," and his teeth rattled together, as he spoke. "I thought there was a great toad under the clothes."

"How foolish you are!"—yet tears were blinding her eyes as she said this. "It's only fancy. Get into bed and shut your eyes. I'll make you another cup of strong coffee. Perhaps that will do you good. You're only a little nervous. Mary's sickness has disturbed you."

Joe looked cautiously under the bedclothes, as he lifted them up still farther, and peered beneath.

"You know there's nothing in your bed; see!"

And Mrs. Morgan threw, with a single jerk, all the clothes upon the floor.

"There now! look for yourself. Now shut your eyes," she continued, as she spread the sheet and quilt over him, after his head was on the pillow. "Shut them tight and keep them so until I boil the water and make a cup of coffee. You know as well as I do that it's nothing but fancy."

Morgan closed his eyes firmly, and drew the clothes over his head.

"I'll be back in a very few minutes," said his wife, going hurriedly to the door. Ere leaving, however, she partly turned her head and glanced back. There sat her husband, upright and staring fearfully.

"Don't, Fanny! don't go away!" he cried. in a frightened voice.

"Joe! Joe! why will you be so foolish? It's nothing but imagination. Now do lie down and shut your eyes. Keep them shut. There now."

And she laid a hand over his eyes, and pressed it down tightly.

"I wish Doctor Green was here," said the wretched man. "He could give me something."

"Shall I go for him?"

"Go, Fanny! Run over right quickly."

"But you won't keep in bed."

"Yes, I will. There now." And he drew the clothes over his face. "There; I'll lie just so until you come back. Now run, Fanny, and don't stay a minute."

Scarcely stopping to think, Mrs. Morgan went hurriedly from the room, and drawing an old shawl over her head, started with swift feet for the residence of Doctor Green, which was not very far away. The kind doctor understood, at a word, the sad condition of her husband, and promised to attend him immediately. Back she flew at even a wilder speed, her heart throbbing with vague apprehension. Oh! what a fearful cry was that which smote her ears as she came within a few paces of home. She knew the voice, changed as it was by terror, and a shudder almost palsied her heart. At a single bound she cleared the intervening space, and in the next moment was in the room where she had left her husband. But he was not there! With suspended breath, and feet that scarcely obeyed her will, she passed into the chamber where little Mary lay. Not here!

"Joe! husband!" she called in a faint voice.

"Here he is, mother." And now she saw that Joe had crept into the bed behind the sick child, and that her arm was drawn tightly around his neck.

"You won't let them hurt me, will you, dear?" said the poor, frightened victim of a terrible mania.

"Nothing will hurt you, father," answered Mary, in a voice that showed her mind to be clear, and fully conscious of her parent's true condition.

She had seen him thus before Ah! what an experience for a child!

"You're an angel—my good angel, Mary," he murmured, in a voice yet trembling with fear. "Pray for me, my child. Oh, ask your Father in heaven to save me from these dreadful creatures. There now!" he cried, rising up suddenly, and looking toward the door. "Keep out! Go away! You can't come in here. This is Mary's room; and she's an angel. Ah, ha! I knew you wouldn't dare come in here—

"A single saint can put to flight,
Ten thousand blustering sons of night."

He added in a half-wandering way, yet with an assured voice, as he laid himself back upon his pillow, and drew the clothes over his head.

"Poor father!" sighed the child, as she gathered both arms about his neck. "I will be your good angel. Nothing shall hurt you here."

"I knew I would be safe where you were," he whispered back—"I knew it, and so I came. Kiss me, love."

How pure and fervent was the kiss laid instantly upon his lips! There was a power in it to remand the evil influences that were surrounding and pressing in upon him like a flood. All was quiet now, and Mrs. Morgan neither by word nor movement disturbed the solemn stillness that reigned in the apartment. In a few minutes the deepened breathing of her husband gave a blessed intimation that he was sinking into sleep. Oh, sleep! sleep! How tearfully, in times past, had she prayed that he might sleep; and yet no sleep came for hours and days—even though powerful opiates were

8

given—until exhausted nature yielded, and
then sleep had a long, long struggle with
death.   Now the sphere of his loving, innocent
child seemed to have overcome, at least for the
time, the evil influences that were getting possession even of his external senses.   Yes, yes,
he was sleeping!   Oh, what a fervent "Thank
God!" went up from the heart of his stricken
wife.

Soon the quick ears of Mrs. Morgan detected
the doctor's approaching footsteps, and she met
him at the door with a finger on her lips.   A
whispered word or two explained the better
aspect of affairs, and the doctor said, encourag-
ingly:

"That's good, if he will only sleep on."

"Do you think he will, doctor?" was asked
anxiously.

"He may.   But we cannot hope too strongly.
It would be something very unusual."

Both passed noiselessly into the chamber.
Morgan still slept, and by his deep breathing

it was plain that he slept soundly. And Mary, too, was sleeping, her face now laid against her father's, and her arms still about his neck. The sight touched even the doctor's heart and moistened his eyes. For nearly half an hour he remained; and then, as Morgan continued to sleep, he left medicine to be given immediately, and went home, promising to call early in the morning.

It is now past midnight, and we leave the lonely, sad-hearted watcher with her sick ones.

———

I was sitting, with a newspaper in my hand —not reading, but musing—at the "Sickle and Sheaf," late in the evening marked by the incidents just detailed.

"Where's your mother?" I heard Simon Slade inquire. He had just entered an adjoining room.

"She's gone out somewhere," was answered by his daughter Flora.

" Where ? "

" I don't know."

" How long has she been away ? "

" More than an hour."

" And you don't know where she went to ? "

" No, sir."

Nothing more was said, but I heard the land-lord's heavy feet moving backward and forward across the room for some minutes.

" Why, Ann! where have you been ? "   The door of the next room had opened and shut.

" Where I wish you had been with me," was answered in a very firm voice.

" Where ? "

" To Joe Morgan's."

" Humph ! "   Only this ejaculation met my ears.   But something was said in a low voice, to which Mrs. Slade replied with some warmth :

" If you don't have his child's blood clinging for life to your garments, you may be thank-ful."

" What do you mean ? " he asked, quickly.

"All that my words indicate. Little Mary is very ill!"

"Well, what of it."

"Much. The doctor thinks her in great danger. The cut on her head has thrown her into a violent fever, and she is delirious. Oh, Simon! if you had heard what I heard to-night."

"What?" was asked in a growling tone.

"She is out of her mind, as I said, and talks a great deal. She talked about you."

"Of me! Well, what had she to say?"

"She said—so pitifully—'I wish Mr. Slade wouldn't look so cross at me. He never did when I went to the mill. He doesn't take me on his knee now, and stroke my hair. Oh, dear!' Poor child! She was always so good."

"Did she say that?" Slade seemed touched.

"Yes, and a great deal more. Once she screamed out, 'Oh, don't! don't, Mr. Slade! don't! My head! my head!' It made my very heart ache. I can never forget her pale,

frightened face, nor her cry of fear. Simon —
if she should die!"

There was a long silence.

"If we were only back to the mill." It was
Mrs. Slade's voice.

"There, now! I don't want to hear that
again," quickly spoke out the landlord. "I
made a slave of myself long enough."

"You had at least a clear conscience," his
wife answered.

"Do hush, will you?" Slade was now angry. "One would think, by the way you talk
sometimes, that I had broken every command
of the Decalogue."

"You will break hearts as well as command-
ments, if you keep on for a few years as you
have begun—and ruin souls as well as fortunes."

Mrs. Slade spoke calmly, but with marked
severity of tone. Her husband answered with
an oath, and then left the room, banging the
door after him. In the hush that followed I
retired to my chamber, and lay for an hour

awake, pondering on all I had just heard. What a revelation was in that brief passage of words between the landlord and his excited companion!

NIGHT THE FOURTH.

DEATH OF LITTLE MARY MORGAN.

"WHERE are you going, Ann?" It was the landlord's voice. Time—a little after dark.

"I'm going over to see Mrs. Morgan," answered his wife.

"What for?"

"I wish to go," was replied.

"Well, *I* don't wish you to go," said Slade, in a very decided way.

"I can't help that, Simon. Mary, I'm told, is dying, and Joe is in a dreadful way. I'm needed there—and so are you, as to that matter. There was a time when, if word came to you that Morgan or his family were in trouble——"

"Do hush, will you!" exclaimed the landlord, angrily. "I won't be preached to in this way any longer."

"Oh, well; then don't interfere with my movements, Simon; that's all I have to say. I'm needed over there, as I just said, and I'm going."

There were considerable odds against him, and Slade, perceiving this, turned off, muttering something that his wife did not hear, and she went on her way. A hurried walk brought her to the wretched home of the poor drunkard, whose wife met her at the door.

"How is Mary?" was the visitor's earnest inquiry.

Mrs. Morgan tried to answer the question; but, though her lips moved, no sounds issued therefrom.

Mrs. Slade pressed her hands tightly in both of hers; and then passed in with her to the room where the child lay. A glance sufficed to tell Mrs. Slade that death had already laid his icy fingers upon her brow.

"How are you, dear?" she asked, as she bent over and kissed her.

"Better, I thank you!" replied Mary, in a low whisper.

Then she fixed her eyes upon her mother's face with a look of inquiry.

"What is it, love?"

"Hasn't father waked up yet?"

"No, dear."

"Won't he wake up soon?"

"He's sleeping very soundly. I wouldn't like to disturb him."

"Oh, no: don't disturb him. I thought, maybe, he was awake."

And the child's lids drooped languidly, until the long lashes lay close against her cheeks.

There was silence for a little while, and then Mrs. Morgan said in a half-whisper to Mrs. Slade:

"Oh, we've had such a dreadful time with poor Joe. He got in that terrible way again last night. I had to go for Doctor Green and leave him all alone. When I came back, he was in bed with Mary; and she, dear child! had her arms around his neck, and was trying to comfort him; and would you believe it, he went off to sleep, and slept in that way for a long time. The doctor came, and when he saw how it was, left some medicine for him, and went away. I was in such hopes that he would sleep it all off. But about twelve o'clock he started up, and sprung out of bed with an awful scream. Poor Mary! she too had fallen asleep. The cry wakened her, and frightened her dreadfully. She's been getting worse ever since, Mrs. Slade.

"Just as he was rushing out of the room, I caught him by the arm, and it took all my strength to hold him.

"'Father! father!' Mary called after him, as soon as she was awake enough to understand what was the matter—'Don't go out, father; there's nothing here.'

" He looked back toward the bed, in a fright
ful way.

"'See, father!' and the dear child turned
down the quilt and sheet, in order to convince
him that nothing was in the bed. 'I'm here,
she added. 'I'm not afraid. Come, father. If
there's nothing here to hurt me, there's nothing
to hurt you.'

"There was something so assuring in this
that Joe took a step or two toward the bed
looking sharply into it as he did so. From
the bed his eyes wandered up to the ceiling
and the old look of terror came into his face.

"'There it is now! Jump out of bed, quick!
Jump out, Mary!' he cried. 'See! it's right
over your head.'

" Mary showed no sign of fear as she lifted
her eyes to the ceiling, and gazed steadily for
a few moments in that direction.

"'There's nothing there, father,' said she, in
a confident voice.

"'It's gone now,' Joe spoke in a tone of re-

"THERE IT IS NOW! JUMP! OUT OF BED, QUICK! JUMP OUT, MARY!
SEE! IT'S RIGHT OVER YOUR HEAD!"

ief. 'Your angel-look drove it away. Aha! There it is now, creeping along the floor!' he suddenly exclaimed, fearfully; starting away from where he stood.

"'Here, father! Here!' Mary called to him, and he sprung into the bed again; while he gathered her arms about him tightly, saying in a low, soothing voice, 'Nothing can harm you here, father.'

" Without a moment's delay, I gave him the morphine left by Doctor Green. He took it eagerly, and then crouched down in the bed, while Mary continued to assure him of perfect safety. So long as he was clearly conscious as to where he was, he remained perfectly still. But, as soon as partial slumber came, he would scream out, and spring from the bed in terror and then it would take us several minutes to quiet him again. Six times during the night did this occur; and as often, Mary coaxed him back. The morphine I continued to give as the doctor had directed. By morning, the opiates had done their work, and he was sleeping soundly. When the doctor came, we removed him to his own bed. He is still asleep; and I begin to feel uneasy, lest he should never awake again. I have heard of this happening."

"See if father isn't awake," said Mary, raising her head from the pillow. She had not heard what passed between her mother and Mrs. Slade, for the conversation was carried on in low voices.

Mrs. Morgan stepped to the door, and looked into the room where her husband lay.

"He is still asleep, dear," she remarked, coming back to the bed.

"Oh! I wish he was awake. I want to see him so much. Won't you call him, mother?"

"I have called him a good many times. But you know the doctor gave him opium. He can't wake up yet."

"He's been sleeping a very long time; don't you think so, mother?"

"Yes, dear, it does seem a long time. But t is best for him. He'll be better when he vakes."

Mary closed her eyes, wearily. How deathly vhite was her face—how sunken her eyes— 1ow sharply contracted her features!

"I've given her up, Mrs. Slade," said Mrs. Morgan, in a low, rough, choking whisper, as he leaned nearer to her friend. "I've given 1er up! The worst is over; but, oh! it seemed 1s though my heart would break in the strug- ;le. Dear child! In all the darkness of my vay, she has helped and comforted me. With- 1ut her, it would have been the blackness of larkness."

"Father! father!" The voice of Mary broke 1ut with a startling quickness.

Mrs. Morgan turned to the bed, and laying 1er hand on Mary's arm said:

"He's still sound asleep, dear."

"No, he isn't, mother. I heard him move. Won't you go in and see if he is awake?"

In order to satisfy the child, her mother lef
the room. To her surprise, she met the eye
of her husband as she entered the chambe
where he lay. He looked at her calmly.

"What does Mary want with me?" h
asked.

"She wishes to see you. She's called yo
so many, many times. Shall I bring her i
here?"

"No. I'll get up and dress myself."

"I wouldn't do that. You've been sick."

"Oh, no. I don't feel sick."

"Father! father!" The clear, earnest voic
of Mary was heard calling.

"I'm coming, dear," answered Morgan.

"Come quick, father, won't you?"

"Yes, love." And Morgan got up an
dressed himself—but with unsteady hands, an
every sign of nervous prostration. In a littl
while, with the assistance of his wife, he wa
ready, and supported by her, came tottering i
to the room where Mary was lying.

"Oh, father!"—What a light broke over her countenance.—"I've been waiting for you so long. I thought you were never going to wake up. Kiss me, father."

"What can I do for you, Mary?" asked Morgan, tenderly, as he laid his face down upon the pillow beside her.

"Nothing, father. I don't wish for anything. I only wanted to see you."

"I'm here, now, love."

"Dear father!" How earnestly, yet tenderly she spoke, laying her small hand upon his face. "You've always been good to me, father."

"Oh, no. I've never been good to anybody," sobbed the weak, broken-spirited man, as he raised himself from the pillow.

How deeply touched was Mrs. Slade, as she sat, the silent witness of this scene!

"You haven't been good to yourself, father— but you've always been good to us."

"Don't, Mary! don't say anything **about**

9

that," interrupted Morgan. "Say that I've been very bad—very wicked. Oh, Mary, dear I only wish that I was as good as you are; I'd like to die, then, and go right away from this evil world. I wish there was no liquor to drink—no taverns—no bar-rooms. Oh dear Oh dear! I wish I was dead."

And the weak, trembling, half-palsied man laid his face again upon the pillow beside his child, and sobbed aloud.

What an oppressive silence reigned for a time through the room!

"Father." The stillness was broken by Mary Her voice was clear and even. "Father, I want to tell you something."

"What is it, Mary?"

"There'll be nobody to go for you, father.' The child's lips now quivered, and tears filled into her eyes.

"Don't talk about that, Mary. I'm not going out in the evening any more until you get well. Don't you remember I promised?"

"But, father"—She hesitated.

"What, dear?"

"I'm going away to leave you and mother."

"Oh, no—no—no, Mary! Don't say that."
—The poor man's voice was broken.—"Don't
say that! We can't let you go, dear."

"God has called me." The child's voice had
a solemn tone, and her eyes turned reverently
upward.

"I wish he would call me! Oh, I wish he
would call me!" groaned Morgan, hiding his
face in his hands. "What shall I do when you
are gone? Oh, dear! Oh, dear!"

"Father!" Mary spoke calmly again. "You
are not ready to go yet. God will let you live
here longer, that you may get ready."

"How can I get ready without you to help
me, Mary? My angel child!"

"Haven't I tried to help you, father, oh, so
many times?" said Mary.

"Yes—yes—you've always tried."

"But it wasn't any use. You would go out

—you would go to the tavern. It seemed almost as if you couldn't help it."

Morgan groaned in spirit.

"Maybe I can help you better, father, after
I die. I love you so much, that I am sure God
will let me come to you, and stay with you always, and be your angel. Don't you think he
will, mother?"

But Mrs. Morgan's heart was too full. She
did not even try to answer, but sat, with streaming eyes, gazing upon her child's face.

"Father, I dreamed something about you,
while I slept to-day." Mary again turned to
her father.

"What was it, dear?"

"I thought it was night, and that I was still
sick. You promised not to go out again until
I was well. But you did go out; and I thought
you went over to Mr. Slade's tavern. When I
knew this, I felt as strong as when I was well,
and I got up and dressed myself, and started
out after you. But I hadn't gone far, before I

met Mr. Slade's great bull-dog, Nero, and he growled at me so dreadfully that I was frightened and ran back home. Then I started again, and went away round by Mr. Mason's. But there was Nero in the road, and this time he caught my dress in his mouth and tore a great piece out of the skirt. I ran back again, and he chased me all the way home. Just as I got to the door, I looked around, and there was Mr. Slade, setting Nero on me. As soon as I saw Mr. Slade, though he looked at me very wicked, I lost all my fear, and turning around, I walked past Nero, who showed his teeth, and growled as fiercely as ever, but didn't touch me. Then Mr. Slade tried to stop me. But I didn't mind him, and kept right on, until I came to the tavern, and there you stood in the door. And you were dressed so nice. You had on a new hat and a new coat; and your boots were new, and polished just like Judge Hammond's. I said: 'O father! is this you?' And then you took me up in your arms and kissed me, and said: 'Yes, Mary, I am your real father. Not old Joe Morgan—but Mr. Morgan now.' It seemed all so strange, that I looked into the bar-room to see who was there. But it wasn't a bar-room any longer; but a store full of goods. The sign of the Sickle and Sheaf was taken down; and over the door I now read your name, father. Oh! I was so glad, that I awoke—and then I cried all to myself, for it was only a dream."

The last words were said very mournfully, and with a drooping of Mary's lids, until the tear-gemmed lashes lay close upon her cheeks. Another period of deep silence followed—for the oppressed listeners gave no utterance to what was in their hearts. Feeling was too strong for speech. Nearly five minutes glided away, and then Mary whispered the name of her father, but without opening her eyes.

Morgan answered, and bent down his ear.

"You will only have mother left," she said

—"only mother. And she cries so much when you are away."

"I won't leave her, Mary, only when I go to work," said Morgan, whispering back to the child. "And I'll never go out at night any more."

"Yes; you promised me that."

"And I'll promise more."

"What, father?"

"Never to go into a tavern again."

"Never!"

"No, never. And I'll promise still more."

"Father?"

"Never to drink a drop of liquor as long as I live."

"Oh, father! dear, dear father!" And with a cry of joy Mary started up and flung herself upon his breast. Morgan drew his arms tightly around her, and sat for a long time, with his lips pressed to her cheek—while she lay against his bosom as still as death. As death? Yes; for, when the father unclasped his arms, the spirit of his child was with the angels of the resurrection !

———

It was my fourth evening in the bar-room of the "Sickle and Sheaf." The company was not large, nor in very gay spirits. All had heard of little Mary's illness; which followed so quickly on the blow from the tumbler, that none hesitated about connecting the one with the other. So regular had been the child's visits, and so gently exerted, yet powerful, her influence over her father, that most of the frequenters at the "Sickle and Sheaf" had felt for her a more than common interest; which the cruel treatment she received, and the subsequent illness, materially heightened.

"Joe Morgan hasn't turned up this evening," remarked some one.

"And isn't likely to for a while," was answered.

"Why not?" inquired the first speaker.

"They say, the man with the poker is after him."

"Oh, dear! that's dreadful. It's the second or third chase, isn't it?"

"Yes."

"He'll be likely to catch him this time."

"I shouldn't wonder."

"Poor devil! It won't be much matter. His family will be a great deal better without him."

"It will be a blessing to them if he dies."

"Miserable, drunken wretch!" muttered Harvey Green, who was present. "He's only in the way of everybody. The sooner he's off, the better."

The landlord said nothing. He stood lean·ing across the bar, looking more sober than usual.

"That was rather an unlucky affair of yours, Simon. They say the child is going to die."

"Who says so?" Slade started, scowled, and threw a quick glance upon the speaker.

"Doctor Green."

"Nonsense! Doctor Green never said any such thing."

"Yes, he did, though."

"Who heard him?"

"I did."

"You did?"

"Yes."

"He wasn't in earnest?" A slight paleness overspread the countenance of the landlord.

"He was, though. They had an awful time there last night."

"Where?"

"At Joe Morgan's. Joe has the mania, and Mrs. Morgan was alone with him and her sick girl all night."

"He deserves to have it; that's all I've got to say." Slade tried to speak with a kind of rough indifference.

"That's pretty hard talk," said one of the company.

"I don't care if it is. It's the truth. What else could he expect?"

"A man like Joe is to be pitied," remarked the other.

"I pity his family," said Slade.

"Especially little Mary." The words were uttered tauntingly, and produced murmurs of satisfaction throughout the room.

Slade started back from where he stood, in an impatient manner, saying something that I did not hear.

"Look here, Simon, I heard some strong suggestions over at Lawyer Phillip's office to-day."

Slade turned his eyes upon the speaker.

"If that child should die, you'll probably have to stand a trial for manslaughter."

"No—girl-slaughter," said Harvey Green, with a cold, inhuman chuckle.

"But, I'm in earnest," said the other. "Mr. Phillips said that a case could be made out of it."

"It was only an accident, and all the lawyers in Christendom can't make anything more of it," remarked Green, taking the side of the landlord, and speaking with more gravity than before.

"Hardly an accident," was replied.

"He didn't throw at the girl."

"No matter. He threw a heavy tumbler at her father's head. The intention was to do an injury; and the law will not stop to make any nice discriminations in regard to the individual upon whom the injury was wrought. Moreover, who is prepared to say that he didn't aim at the girl?"

"Any man who intimates such a thing is a cursed liar!" exclaimed the landlord, half maddened by the suggestion.

"I won't throw a tumbler at your head," coolly remarked the individual whose plain speaking had so irritated Simon Slade. "Throwing tumblers I never thought a very creditable kind of argument—though with some men, when cornered, it is a favorite mode of settling a question. Now, as for our friend the landlord, I am sorry to say that his new business doesn't seem to have improved either his manners or his temper a great deal. As a miller, he was one of the best-tempered men in the world, and wouldn't have harmed a kitten. But, now, he can swear, and bluster, and throw glasses at people's heads, and all that sort of thing, with the best of brawling rowdies. I'm afraid he's taking lessons in a bad school—I am."

"I don't think you have any right to insult a man in his own house," answered Slade, in a voice dropped to a lower key than the one in which he had before spoken.

"I had no intention to insult you," said the other. "I was only speaking suppositiously, and in view of your position on a trial for manslaughter, when I suggested that no one could prove, or say that you didn't mean to strike little Mary, when you threw the tumbler."

"Well, I didn't mean to strike her: and I

don't believe there is a man in this bar-room
who thinks that I did—not one."

"I'm sure I do not," said the individual with
whom he was in controversy. "Nor I"—"Nor
I"—went round the room.

"But, as I wished to set forth," was continued, "the case will not be so plain a one when
it finds its way into court, and twelve men, to
each of whom you may be a stranger, come to
sit in judgment upon the act. The slightest
twist in the evidence, the prepossessions of a
witness, or the bad tact of the prosecution, may
cause things to look so dark on your side as to
leave you but little chance. For my part, if
the child should die, I think your chances
for a term in the state's prison are as eight
to ten; and I should call that pretty close
cutting."

I looked attentively at the man who said
this, all the while he was speaking, but could
not clearly make out whether he were altogether in earnest, or merely trying to worry

the mind of Slade. That he was successful in accomplishing the latter, was very plain; for the landlord's countenance steadily lost color, and became overcast with alarm. With that evil delight which some men take in giving pain, others, seeing Slade's anxious looks, joined in the persecution, and soon made the landlord's case look black enough; and the landlord himself almost as frightened as a criminal just under arrest.

"It's bad business, and no mistake," said one.

"Yes, bad enough. I wouldn't be in his shoes for his coat," remarked another.

"For his coat? No, not for his whole wardrobe," said a third.

"Nor for the Sickle and Sheaf thrown into the bargain," added a fourth.

"It will be a clear case of manslaughter, and no mistake. What is the penalty?"

"From two to ten years in the penitentiary," was readily answered.

"They'll give him five, I reckon."

"No—not more than two. It will be hard to prove malicious intention."

"I don't know that. I've heard him curse the girl and threaten her many a time. Haven't you?"

"Yes "—"Yes "—"I have, often," ran around the bar-room.

"You'd better hang me at once," said Slade, affecting to laugh.

At this moment, the door behind Slade opened, and I saw his wife's anxious face thrust in for a moment. She said something to her husband, who uttered a low ejaculation of surprise, and went out quickly.

"What's the matter now?" asked one of another.

"I shouldn't wonder if little Mary Morgan was dead," was suggested.

"I heard her say dead," remarked one who was standing near the bar.

"What's the matter, Frank?" inquired several voices, as the landlord's son came in through the door out of which his father had passed.

"Mary Morgan is dead," answered the boy.

"Poor child! Poor child!" sighed one, in genuine regret at the not unlooked for intelligence. "Her trouble is over."

And there was not one present, but Harvey Green, who did not utter some word of pity or sympathy. He shrugged his shoulders, and looked as much of contempt and indifference as he thought it prudent to express.

"See here, boys," spoke out one of the company, "can't we do something for poor Mrs. Morgan? Can't we make up a purse for her?"

"That's it," was quickly responded; "I'm good for three dollars; and there they are," drawing out the money and laying it upon the counter.

"And here are five to go with them," said I, quickly stepping forward, and placing a five-dollar bill alongside of the first contribution.

"Here are five more," added a third indi-

10

vidual. And so it went on, until thirty dollars were paid down for the benefit of Mrs. Morgan.

"Into whose hands shall this be placed?" was next asked.

"Let me suggest Mrs. Slade," said I. "To my certain knowledge, she has been with Mrs. Morgan to-night. I know that she feels in her a true woman's interest."

"Just the person," was answered. "Frank, tell your mother we would like to see her. Ask her to step into the sitting-room."

In a few moments the boy came back, and said that his mother would see us in the next room, into which we all passed. Mrs. Slade stood near the table, on which burned a lamp. I noticed that her eyes were red, and that there was on her countenance a troubled and sorrowful expression.

"We have just heard," said one of the company, that little Mary Morgan is dead."

"Yes—it is too true," answered Mrs. Slade,

mournfully. "I have just left there. Poor child! she has passed from an evil world."

"Evil it has indeed been to her," was remarked.

"You may well say that. And yet, amid all the evil, she has been an angel of mercy. Her last thought in dying was of her miserable father. For him, at any time, she would have laid down her life willingly."

"Her mother must be nearly broken-hearted. Mary is the last of her children."

"And yet the child's death may prove a blessing to her."

"How so?"

"Her father promised Mary, just at the last moment—solemnly promised her—that, henceforth, he would never taste liquor. That was all her trouble. That was the thorn in her dying pillow. But he plucked it out, and she went to sleep, lying against his heart. Oh, gentlemen! it was the most touching sight I ever saw."

All present seemed deeply moved.

"They are very poor and wretched," was said.

"Poor and miserable enough," answered Mrs. Slade.

"We have just been taking up a collection for Mrs. Morgan. Here is the money, Mrs. Slade—thirty dollars—we place it in your hands for her benefit. Do with it, for her, as you may see best."

"Oh, gentlemen!" What a quick gleam went over the face of Mrs. Slade. "I thank you, from my heart, in the name of that unhappy one, for this act of true benevolence. To you the sacrifice has been small; to her the benefit will be great indeed. A new life will, I trust, be commenced by her husband, and this timely aid will be something to rest upon, until he can get into better employment than he now has. Oh, gentlemen! let me urge on you, one and all, to make common cause in favor of Joe Morgan. His purposes are good now; he means to keep his promise to his dying child—means to reform his life. Let the good impulses that led to this act of relief further prompt you to watch over him, and, if you see him about going astray, to lead him kindly back into the right path.—Never—oh! never encourage him to drink; but rather take the glass from his hand, if his own appetite lead him aside, and by all the persuasive influence you possess, induce him to go out from the place of temptation.

"Pardon my boldness in saying so much." added Mrs. Slade, recollecting herself, and coloring deeply as she did so. "My feelings have led me away."

And she took the money from the table where it had been placed, and retired toward the door.

"You have spoken well, madam," was answered. "And we thank you for reminding us of our duty."

"One word more—and forgive the earnest heart from which it comes"—said Mrs. Slade,

in a voice that trembled on the words she uttered. "I cannot help speaking, gentlemen!
Think if some of you be not entering the road
wherein Joe Morgan has so long been walking.
Save him, in heaven's name!—but see that ye
do not yourselves become cast-aways!"

As she said this. she glided through the door.
and it closed after her.

"I don't know what her husband would say
to that," was remarked after a few moments of
surprised silence.

"I don't care what *he* would say; but I'll
tell you what *I* will say," spoke out a man
whom I had several times noticed as rather a
free tippler. "The old lady has given us capital advice, and I mean to take it, for one. I'm
going to try to save Joe Morgan, and—myself
too. I've already entered the road she referred
to; but I'm going to turn back. So good-night
to you all; and if Simon Slade gets no more of
my sixpences, he may thank his wife for it—
God bless her?"

And the man drew his hat with a jerk over his forehead, and left immediately.

This seemed the signal for dispersion, and all retired—not by way of the bar-room, but out into the hall, and through the door leading upon the porch that ran along in front of the house. Soon after the bar was closed, and a dead silence reigned throughout the house. I saw no more of Slade that night. Early in the morning, I left Cedarville; the landlord looked very sober when he bade me good-by through the stage-door, and wished me a pleasant journey.

NIGHT THE FIFTH.

SOME OF THE CONSEQUENCES OF TAVERN-KEEPING.

NEARLY five years glided away before business again called me to Cedarville. I knew little of what passed there in the interval, except that Simon Slade had actually been indicted for manslaughter, in causing the death of Morgan's child. He did not stand a trial, however, Judge Lyman having used his influence, successfully, in getting the indictment quashed. The judge, some people said, interested himself in Slade more than was just seemly—especially, as he had, on several occasions, in the discharge of his official duties, displayed what seemed an over-righteous indignation against individuals arraigned for petty offences. The impression made upon me by Judge Lyman had not been favorable. He seemed a cold, selfish, scheming man of the world. That he was an unscrupulous politician, was plain to me, in a single evening's observation of his sayings and doings among the common herd of a village bar-room.

As the stage rolled, with a gay flourish of our driver's bugle, into the village, I noted here and there familiar objects, and marked the varied evidences of change. Our way was past the elegant residence and grounds of Judge Hammond, the most beautiful and highly cultivated in Cedarville. At least, such it was regarded at the time of my previous visit. But, the moment my eyes rested upon the dwelling and its varied surroundings, I perceived an altered aspect. Was it the simple work of time? or, had familiarity with other and more elegantly arranged suburban homes, marred this in my eyes by involuntary contrast? Or had the hand of cultivation really been stayed, and the marring fingers of neglect suffered undisturbed to trace on every thing disfiguring characters?.

Such questions were in my thoughts, when I saw a man in the large portico of the dwelling, the ample columns of which, capped in rich Corinthian, gave the edifice the aspect of a Grecian temple. He stood leaning against one of the columns—his hat off, and his long gray hair thrown back and resting lightly on his neck and shoulders. His head was bent down upon his breast, and he seemed in deep abstraction. Just as the coach swept by, he looked up, and in the changed features I recognized Judge Hammond. His complexion was still florid, but his face had grown thin, and his eyes were sunken. Trouble was written in every lineament. Trouble? How inadequately does the word express my meaning! Ah! at a single glance, what a volume of suffering was opened to the gazer's eye. Not lightly had the foot of time rested there, as if treading on odorous flowers, but heavily, and with iron-shod heel. This I saw at a glance; and then, only the image of the man was present to my inner vision, for the swiftly rolling stage-coach had borne me onward past the altered home of the wealthiest denizen of Cedarville. In a few minutes our driver reined up before the "Sickle and Sheaf," and as I stepped to the ground, a rotund, coarse, red-faced man, whom I failed to recognize as Simon Slade until he spoke, grasped my hand, and pronounced my name. I could not but contrast, in thought, his appearance with what it was when I first saw him, some six years previously; nor help saying to myself:

"So much for tavern-keeping!"

As marked a change was visible everywhere in and around the "Sickle and Sheaf." It, too, had grown larger by additions of wings and rooms; but it had also grown coarser in growing larger. When built, all the doors were painted white, and the shutters green, giving to the house a neat, even tasteful appearance. But the white and green had given place to a dark, dirty brown, that to my eyes was particularly unattractive. The bar-room had been extended, and now a polished brass rod, or railing, embellished the counter, and sundry ornamental attractions had been given to the shelving behind the bar—such as mirrors, gilding, etc. Pictures, too, were hung upon the walls, or more accurately speaking, coarse colored lithographs, the subjects of which, if not really obscene, were flashing, or vulgar. In the sitting-room, next to the bar, I noticed little change of objects, but much in their condition. The carpet, chairs, and tables were the same in fact, but far from being the same in appearance. The room had a close, greasy odor, and looked as if it had not been thoroughly swept and dusted for a week.

A smart young Irishman was in the bar, and handed me the book in which passenger's names were registered. After I had recorded mine, he directed my trunk to be carried to the room designated as the one I was to occupy. I followed the porter, who conducted me to the chamber which had been mine at previous visits. Here, too, were evidences of change; but not for the better. Then the room was as sweet and clean as it could be; the sheets and pillow-cases as white as snow, and the furniture shining with polish. Now all was dusty and dingy, the air foul, and the bed-linen scarcely whiter than tow. No curtain made softer the light as it came through the window; nor would the shutters entirely keep out the glare, for several of the slats were broken. A feeling of disgust came over me, at the close smell and foul appearance of everything; so, after washing my hands and face, and brushing the dust from my clothes, I went down-stairs. The sitting-room was scarcely more attractive than my chamber; so I went out upon the porch and took a chair. Several loungers were here; hearty, strong-looking, but lazy fellows, who, if they had anything to do, liked idling better than working. One of them had leaned his chair back against the wall of the house, and

was swinging his legs with a half circular motion, and humming "Old Folks at Home."
Another set astride of his chair, with his face
turned toward, and his chin resting upon, the
back. He was in too lazy a condition of body
and mind for motion or singing. A third had
slidden down in his chair, until he sat on his
back, while his feet were elevated above his
head, and resting against one of the pillars that
supported the porch; while a fourth lay
stretched out on a bench, sleeping, his hat over
his face to protect him from buzzing and biting
flies.

Though all but the sleeping man eyed me in-
quisitively, as I took my place among them, not
one changed his position. The rolling of eye-
balls cost but little exertion; and with that
effort they were contented.

"Hallo! who's that?" one of these loungers
suddenly exclaimed, as a man went swiftly by
in a light sulky; and he started up, and gazed
down the road, seeking to penetrate the cloud

of dust which the fleet rider had swept up with hoofs and wheels.

"I didn't see." The sleeping man aroused himself, rubbed his eyes, and gazed along the road.

"Who was it, Matthew?" The Irish bar-keeper now stood in the door.

"Willy Hammond," was answered by Matthew.

"Indeed! Is that his new three hundred dollar horse?"

"Yes."

"My! but he's a screamer!"

"Isn't he! Most as fast as his young master."

"Hardly," said one of the men, laughing. "I don't think anything in creation can beat Hammond. He goes it with a perfect rush."

"Doesn't he! Well; you may say what you please of him, he's as good-hearted a fellow as ever walked; and generous to a fault."

"His old dad will agree with you in the last remark," said Matthew.

"No doubt of that, for he has to stand the bills," was answered.

"Yes, whether he will or no, for I rather think Willy has, somehow or other, got the upper hand of him."

"In what way?"

"It's Hammond and Son, over at the mill and distillery."

"I know; but what of that!"

"Willy was made the business man—ostensibly—in order, as the old man thought, to get him to feel the responsibility of the new position, and thus tame him down."

"Tame *him* down! Oh, dear! It will take more than business to do that. The curb was applied too late."

"As the old gentleman has already discovered, I'm thinking, to his sorrow."

"He never comes here any more; does he, Matthew?"

"Who?"

"Judge Hammond."

"Oh, dear, no. He and Slade had all sorts of a quarrel about a year ago, and he's never darkened our doors since."

"It was something about Willy and ——." The speaker did not mention any name, but winked knowingly and tossed his head toward the entrance of the house, to indicate some member of Slade's family.

"I believe so."

"D'ye think Willy really likes her?"

Matthew shrugged his shoulders, but made no answer.

"She's a nice girl," was remarked in an under tone, and good enough for Hammond's son any day; though, if she were my daughter, I'd rather see her in Jericho than fond of his company."

"He'll have plenty of money to give her. She can live like a queen."

"For how long?"
11

"Hush!" came from the lips of Matthew. "There she is now."

I looked up, and saw at a short distance from the house, and approaching, a young lady, in whose sweet, modest face, I at once recognized Flora Slade. Five years had developed her into a beautiful woman. In her alone, of all that appertained to Simon Slade, there was no deterioration. Her eyes were as mild and pure as when first I met her at gentle sixteen, and her father said "My daughter," with such a mingling of pride and affection in his tone. She passed near where I was sitting, and entered the house. A closer view showed me some marks of thought and suffering; but they only heightened the attractions of her face. I failed not to observe the air of respect with which all returned her slight nod and smile of recognition.

"She's a nice girl, and no mistake—the flower of this flock," was said, as soon as she passed into the house.

"Too good for Willy Hammond, in my opinion," said Matthew. "Clever and generous as people call him."

"Just my opinion," was responded. "She's as pure and good, almost, as an angel; and he? —I can tell you what—he's not the clear thing. He knows a little too much of the world—on its bad side, I mean."

The appearance of Slade put an end to this conversation. A second observation of his person and countenance did not remove the first unfavorable impression. His face had grown decidedly bad in expression, as well as gross and sensual. The odor of his breath, as he took a chair close to where I was sitting, was that of one who drank habitually and freely; and the red, swimming eyes evidenced, too surely, a ripid progress toward the sad condition of a confirmed inebriate. There was, too, a certain thickness of speech, that gave another corroborating sign of evil progress.

"Have you seen anything of Frank this afternoon?" he inquired of Matthew, after we had passed a few words.

"Nothing," was the bar-keeper's answer.

"I saw him with Tom Wilkins as I came over," said one of the men who was sitting in the porch.

"What was he doing with Tom Wilkins?" said Slade, in a fretted tone of voice. "He doesn't seem very choice of his company."

"They were gunning."

"Gunning!"

"Yes. They both had fowling-pieces. I wasn't near enough to ask where they were going."

This information disturbed Slade a good deal. After muttering to himself a little while, he started up and went into the house.

"And I could have told him a little more, had I been so inclined," said the individual who mentioned the fact that Frank was with Tom Wilkins.

"What more?" inquired Matthew.

"There was a buggy in the case; and a champagne basket. What the latter contained you can easily guess."

"Whose buggy?"

"I don't know anything about the buggy; but if 'Lightfoot' doesn't sink in value a hundred dollars or so before sundown, call me a false prophet."

"Oh, no," said Matthew, incredulously. "Frank wouldn't do an outrageous thing like that. Lightfoot won't be in a condition to drive for a month to come."

"I don't care. She's out now; and the way she was putting it down when I saw her, would have made a locomotive look cloudy."

"Where did he get her?" was inquired.

"She's been in the six-acre field, over by Mason's Bridge, for the last week or so," Matthew answered. "Well; all I have to say," he added, "is that Frank ought to be slung up and well horse-whipped. I never saw such a young rascal. He cares for no good, and fears no evil. He's the worst boy I ever saw."

"It would hardly do for you to call him a boy to his face," said one of the men, laughing.

"I don't have much to say to him in any way," replied Matthew, "for I know very well that if we ever do get into a regular quarrel, there'll be a hard time of it. The same house will not hold us afterward—that's certain. So I steer clear of the young reprobate."

"I wonder his father don't put him to some business," was remarked. "The idle life he now leads will be his ruin."

"He was behind the bar for a year or two."

"Yes; and was smart at mixing a glass— but——"

"Was himself becoming too good a cus- tomer?"

"Precisely. He got drunk as a fool before reaching his fifteenth year."

"Good gracious!" I exclaimed, involun- tarily.

"It's true, sir," said the last speaker, turning to me, "I never saw anything like it. And this wasn't all bar-room talk, which, as you may know, isn't the most refined and virtuous in the world. I wouldn't like my son to hear much of it. Frank was always an eager listener to everything that was said, and in a very short time became an adept in slang and profanity. I'm no saint myself; but it's often made my blood run cold to hear him swear."

"I pity his mother," said I; for my thought turned naturally to Mrs. Slade.

"You may well do that," was answered. "I doubt if Cedarville holds a sadder heart. It was a dark day for her, let me tell you, when Simon Slade sold his mill and built this tavern. She was opposed to it in the beginning."

"I have inferred as much."

"I know it," said the man. "My wife has been intimate with her for years. Indeed, they have always been like sisters. I remember very well her coming to our house, about the time the mill was sold, and crying about it as if her heart would break. She saw nothing but trouble and sorrow ahead. Tavern-keeping she had always regarded as a low business; and the change from a respectable miller to a lazy tavern-keeper, as she expressed it, was presented to her mind as something disgraceful. I remember, very well, trying to argue the point with her—assuming that it was quite as respectable to keep tavern as to do anything else; but I might as well have talked to the wind. She was always a pleasant, hopeful, cheerful woman before that time; but, really, I don't think I've seen a true smile on her face since."

"That was a great deal for a man to lose," said I.

"What?" he inquired, not clearly understanding me.

"The cheerful face of his wife."

"The face was but an index of her heart," said he.

"So much the worse."

"True enough for that. Yes, it was a great deal to lose."

"What has he gained that will make up for this?"

The man shrugged his shoulders.

"What has he gained?" I repeated. "Can you figure it up?"

"He's a richer man, for one thing."

"Happier?"

There was another shrug of the shoulders.
"I wouldn't like to say that."

"How much richer?"

"Oh, a great deal. Somebody was saying, only yesterday, that he couldn't be worth less than thirty thousand dollars."

"Indeed? So much."

"Yes."

"How has he managed to accumulate so rapidly?"

"His bar has a large run of custom. And, you know, that pays wonderfully."

"He must have sold a great deal of liquor in six years."

"And he has. I don't think I'm wrong in saying that in the six years which have gone by since the 'Sickle and Sheaf' was opened, more liquor has been drank than in the previous twenty years."

"Say forty," remarked a man who had been a listener to what we said.

"Let it be forty then," was the according answer.

"How comes this?" I inquired. "You had a tavern here before the Sickle and Sheaf was opened."

"I know we had, and several places besides, where liquor was sold. But, everybody far and near knew Simon Slade the miller, and everybody liked him. He was a good miller, and a cheerful, social, chatty sort of a man, putting everybody in a good humor who came near him. So it became the talk everywhere, when he built this house, which he fitted up nicer than anything that had been seen in these parts. Judge Hammond, Judge Lyman, Lawyer Wilson, and all the big-bugs of the place at once patronized the new tavern; and, of course, everybody else did the same. So, you can easily see how he got such a run."

"It was thought, in the beginning," said I, "that the new tavern was going to do wonders for Cedarville."

"Yes," answered the man laughing, "and so it has."

"In what respect?"

"Oh, in many. It has made some men richer, and some poorer."

"Who has it made poorer?"

"Dozens of people. You may always take it for granted, when you see a tavern-keeper who has a good run at his bar, getting rich, that a great many people are getting poor."

"How so?" I wished to hear in what way the man, who was himself, as was plain to see, a good customer at somebody's bar, reasoned on the subject.

"He does not add to the general wealth. He produces nothing. He takes money from his customers, but gives them no article of value in return—nothing that can be called property, personal or real. He is just so much richer and they just so much poorer for the exchange. Is it not so?"

I readily assented to the position as true, and then said—

"Who, in particular, is poorer?"

"Judge Hammond, for one."

"Indeed! I thought the advance in his property, in consequence of the building of this tavern, was so great, that he was reaping a rich pecuniary harvest."

"There was a slight advance in property along the street after the Sickle and Sheaf was opened, and Judge Hammond was benefited thereby. Interested parties made a good deal of noise about it; but it didn't amount to much, I believe."

"What has caused the judge to grow poorer?"

"The opening of this tavern, as I just said."

"In what way did it affect him?"

"He was among Slade's warmest supporters, as soon as he felt the advance in the price of building lots, called him one of the most enterprising men in Cedarville—a real benefactor to the place—and all that stuff. To set a good example of patronage, he came over every day and took his glass of brandy, and encouraged everybody else that he could influence to do the same. Among those who followed his example was his son Willy. There was not, let me tell you, in all the country for twenty miles around, a finer young man than Willy, nor one of so much promise, when this man-trap"—he let his voice fall, and glanced around, as he thus designated Slade's tavern—"was opened; and now, there is not one dashing more recklessly along the road to ruin. When too late, his father saw that his son was corrupted, and that the company he kept was of a dangerous character. Two reasons led him to purchase Slade's old mill, and turn it into a factory and a distillery. Of course, he had to make a heavy outlay for additional buildings, machinery, and distilling apparatus. The reasons influencing him were the prospect of realizing a large amount of money, especially in distilling, and the hope of saving Willy, by getting him closely engaged and interested in business. To accomplish, more certainly, the latter end, he unwisely transferred to his son, as his own capital, twenty thousand dollars, and then formed with him a regular copartnership— giving Willy an active business control.

"But the experiment, sir," added the man, emphatically, "has proved a failure. I heard yesterday, that both mill and distillery were to be shut up, and offered for sale."

"They did not prove as money-making as was anticipated?"

"No, not under Willy Hammond's manage-

ment. He had made too many bad acquaint-
ances—men who clung to him because he had
plenty of money at his command, and spent it
as freely as water. One-half of his time he was
away from the mill, and while there, didn't half
attend to business. I've heard it said—and I
don't much doubt its truth—that he's squandered his twenty thousand dollars, and a great
deal more besides."

"How is that possible?"

"Well; people talk, and not always at random. There's been a man staying here, most
of his time, for the last four or five years, named
Green. He does not do any thing, and don't
seem to have any friends in the neighborhood.
Nobody knows where he came from, and he is
not at all communicative on that head himself.
Well, this man became acquainted with young
Hammond after Willy got to visiting the bar
here, and attached himself to him at once. They
have, to all appearance, been fast friends ever
since; riding about, or going off on gunning or

fishing excursions almost every day, and seclud·
ing themselves somewhere nearly every even·
ing. That man, Green, sir, it is whispered, is a
gambler; and I believe it. Granted, and there
is no longer a mystery as to what Willy does
with his own and his father's money."

I readily assented to this view of the case.

"And so assuming that Green is a gambler,"
said I, "he has grown richer, in consequence of
the opening of a new and more attrative tavern
in Cedarville."

"Yes, and Cedarville is so much the poorer
for all his gains; for I've never heard of his
buying a foot of ground, or in any way encour-
aging productive industry. He's only a blood-
sucker."

"It is worse than the mere abstraction of
money," I remarked; "he corrupts his victims,
at the same time that he robs them."

"True."

"Willy Hammond may not be his only vic·
tim," I suggested.

"Nor is he, in my opinion. I've been coming to this bar, nightly, for a good many years—a sorry confession for a man to make, I must own," he added, with a slight tinge of shame; "but so it is. Well, as I was saying, I've been coming to this bar, nightly, for a good many years, and I generally see all that is going on around me. Among the regular visitors are at least half a dozen young men, belonging to our best families—who have been raised with care, and well educated. That their presence here is unknown to their friends, I am quite certain —or, at least, unknown and unsuspected by some of them. They do not drink a great deal yet; but all try a glass or two. Toward nine o'clock, often at an earlier hour, you will see one and another of them go quietly out of the bar, through the sitting-room, preceded, or soon followed, by Green and Slade. At any hour of the night, up to one or two, and sometimes three o'clock, you can see light streaming through the rent in a curtain drawn before a

12

particular window, which I know to be in the
room of Harvey Green. These are facts, sir;
and you can draw your own conclusion. I
think it a very serious matter."

"Why does Slade go out with these young
men?" I inquired. "Do you think he gambles
also?"

"If he isn't a kind of a stool-pigeon for Har.
vey Green, then I'm mistaken again."

"Hardly. He cannot, already, have become
so utterly unprincipled."

"It's a bad school, sir, this tavern-keeping,"
said the man.

"I readily grant you that."

"And it's nearly seven years since he commenced to take lessons. A great deal may be
learned, sir, of good or evil, in seven years,
especially if any interest be taken in the
studies."

"True."

"And it's true in this case, you may depend
upon it. Simon Slade is not the man he was,

seven years ago. Anybody with half an eye
can see that. He's grown selfish, grasping, unscrupulous, and passionate. There could hardly
be a greater difference between men than exists
between Simon Slade the tavern-keeper, and
Simon Slade the miller."

"And intemperate, also?" I suggested.

"He's beginning to take a little too much,"
was answered.

"In that case, he'll scarcely be as well off five
years hence as he is now."

"He's at the top of the wheel, some of us
think."

"What has led to this opinion?"

"He's beginning to neglect his house, for one
thing."

"A bad sign."

"And there is another sign. Heretofore, he
has always been on hand, with the cash, when
desirable property went off, under forced sale,
at a bargain. In the last three or four months,
several great sacrifices have been made, but

Simon Slade showed no inclination to buy. Put this fact against another,—week before last, he sold a house and lot in the town for five hundred dollars less than he paid for them, a year ago—and for just that sum less than their true value."

"How came that?" I inquired.

"Ah! there's the question! He wanted money; though for what purpose he has not intimated to any one, as far as I can learn."

"What do you think of it?"

"Just this. He and Green have been hunting together in times past; but the professed gambler's instincts are too strong to let him spare even his friend in evil. They have commenced playing one against the other."

"Ah! you think so?"

"I do; and if I conjecture rightly, Simon Slade will be a poorer man, in a year from this time, than he is now."

Here our conversation was interrupted. Some one asked my talkative friend to go and take a drink, and he, nothing loath, left me without ceremony.

Very differently served was the supper I partook of on that evening, from the one set before me on the occasion of my first visit to the "Sickle and Sheaf." The table-cloth was not merely soiled, but offensively dirty; the plates, cups, and saucers, dingy and sticky; the knives and forks unpolished; and the food of a character to satisfy the appetite with a very few mouthfuls. Two greasy-looking Irish girls waited on the table, at which neither landlord nor landlady presided. I was really hungry when the supper-bell rang; but the craving of my stomach soon ceased in the atmosphere of the dining-room, and I was the first to leave the table.

Soon after the lamps were lighted, company began to assemble in the spacious bar-room, where were comfortable seats, with tables, newspapers, backgammon boards, dominoes, etc. The first act of nearly every one who

came in was to call for a glass of liquor; and
sometimes the same individual drank two or
three times in the course of half an hour, on
the invitation of new comers who were con-
vivially inclined.

Most of those who came in were strangers to
me. I was looking from face to face to see if
any of the old company were present, when
one countenance struck me as familiar. I was
studying it, in order, if possible, to identify
the person, when some one addressed him as
"Judge."

Changed as the face was, I now recognized
it as that of Judge Lyman. Five years had
marred that face terribly. It seemed twice the
former size; and all its bright expression was
gone. The thickened and protruding eyelids
half closed the leaden eyes, and the swollen
lips and cheeks gave to his countenance a look
of all-predominating sensuality. True manli-
ness had bowed itself in debasing submission
to the bestial. He talked loudly, and with a

pompous dogmatism—mainly on political subjects—but talked only from memory; for any
one could see, that thought came into but feeble
activity. And yet, derationalized, so to speak,
as he was, through drink, he had been chosen
a representative in Congress, at the previous
election, on the anti-temperance ticket, and by
a very handsome majority. He was the rum
candidate; and the rum interest, aided by the
easily swayed "indifferents," swept aside the
claims of law, order, temperance, and good
morals; and the district from which he was
chosen as a National Legislator sent him up to
the National Councils, and said in the act—
"Look upon him we have chosen as our representative, and see in him a type of our principles, our quality, and our condition as a community."

Judge Lyman, around whom a little circle
soon gathered, was very severe on the temperance party, which, for two years, had opposed
his election, and which, at the last struggle,

showed itself to be a rapidly growing organiza-
tion. During the canvass, a paper was published by this party, in which his personal
habits, character, and moral principles were
discussed in the freest manner, and certainly
not in a way to elevate him in the estimation
of men whose opinion was of any value.

It was not much to be wondered at, that he
assumed to think temperance issues at the polls
were false issues; and that when temperance
men sought to tamper with elections, the liberties of the people were in danger; nor that
he pronounced the whole body of temperance
men as selfish schemers and canting hypocrites.

"The next thing we will have," he exclaimed,
warming with his theme, and speaking so loud
that his voice sounded throughout the room,
and arrested every one's attention, "will be
laws to fine any man who takes a chew of to-
bacco, or lights a cigar. Touch the liberties of
the people in the smallest particular, and all
guarantees are gone. The Stamp Act, against

which our noble forefathers rebelled, was a light measure of oppression to that contemplated by these worse than fanatics."

"You are right there, judge; right for once in your life, if you (hic) were never right before!" exclaimed a battered looking specimen of humanity, who stood near the speaker, slapping Judge Lyman on the shoulder familiarly as he spoke. "There's no telling what they will do. There's (hic) my old uncle Josh Wilson, who's been keeper of the Poor-house these ten years. Well, they're going to turn him out, if ever they get the upper hand in Bolton county."

"If? That word involves a great deal, Harry!" said Lyman. "We mus'n't let them get the upper hand. Every man has a duty to perform to his country in this matter, and every one must do his duty. But what have they got against your Uncle Joshua? What has he been doing to offend this righteous party?"

"They've nothing against him, (hic) I be-lieve. Only, they say, they're not going to have a Poor-house in the county at all."

"What! Going to turn the poor wretches out to starve?" said one.

"Oh no! (hic)," and the fellow grinned, half shrewdly and half maliciously, as he answered —"no, not that. But, when they carry the day, there'll be no need of Poor-houses. At least, that's their talk—and I guess maybe there's something in it, for I never knew a man to go to the Poor-house, who hadn't (hic) rum to blame for his poverty. But, you see, I'm interested in this matter. I go for keeping up the Poor-house (hic); for I guess I'm traveling that road, and I shouldn't like to get to the last milestone (hic) and find no snug quarters —no Uncle Josh. You're safe for one vote, any how, old chap, on next election day!" And the man's broad hand slapped the mem-ber's shoulder again. "Huzza for the rum-mies! That's (hic) the ticket! Harry

"HUZZA FOR THE RUMMIES! THAT'S THE TICKET!"

Grimes never deserts his friends. True as steel!"

"You're a trump!" returned Judge Lyman, with low familiarity. "Never fear about the Poor-house and Uncle Josh. They're all safe."

"But look here, judge," resumed the man. "It isn't only the Poor-house, the jail is to go next."

"Indeed!"

"Yes, that's their talk; and I guess they ain't far out of the way neither. What takes men to jail? You can tell us something about that, judge, for you've jugged a good many in your time. Didn't pretty much all of 'em drink rum? (hic.)"

But the judge answered nothing.

"Silence (hic) gives consent," resumed Grimes. "And they say more; once give 'em the upper hand—and they're confident of beating us—and the Court-house will be to let. As for judges and lawyers, they'll starve, or go into some better business. So you see, (hic) judge, your liberties are in danger. But fight hard, old fellow; and if you must die, (hic) die game!"

How well Judge Lyman relished this mode of presenting the case, was not very apparent; he was too good a politician and office-seeker, to show any feeling on the subject, and thus endanger a vote. Harry Grimes' vote counted one, and a single vote sometimes gained or lost an election.

"One of their gags," he said, laughing. "But I'm too old a stager not to see the flimsiness of such pretensions. Poverty and crime have their origin in the corrupt heart, and their foundations are laid long and long before the first step is taken on the road to inebriety. It is easy to promise results; for only the few look at causes, and trace them to their effects."

"Rum and ruin, (hic). Are they not cause and effect?" asked Grimes.

"Sometimes they are," was the half extorted answer.

"Oh, Green, is that you?" exclaimed the judge, as Harvey Green came in with a soft cat-like step. He was, evidently, glad of a chance to get rid of his familiar friend and elector.

I turned my eyes upon the man, and read his face closely. It was unchanged. The same cold, sinister eye; the same chiselled mouth, so firm now, and now yielding so elastically; the same smile "from the teeth outward"—the same lines that revealed his heart's deep, dark selfishness. If he had indulged in drink during the five intervening years, it had not corrupted his blood, nor added thereto a single degree of heat.

"Have you seen anything of Hammond this evening?" asked Judge Lyman.

"I saw him an hour or two ago," answered Green.

"How does he like his new horse?"

"He's delighted with him."

"What was the price?"

"Three hundred dollars."

"Indeed!"

The judge had already arisen, and he and Green were now walking side by side across the bar-room floor.

"I want to speak a word with you," I heard Lyman say.

And then the two went out together. I saw no more of them during the evening.

Not long afterward, Willy Hammond came in. Ah! there was a sad change here; a change that in no way belied the words of Matthew the bar-keeper. He went up to the bar, and I heard him ask for Judge Lyman. The answer was in so low a voice that it did not reach my ear.

With a quick, nervous motion, Hammond threw his hand toward a row of decanters on the shelf behind the bar-keeper, who immediately set one of them containing brandy before him. From this he poured a tumbler half full, and drank it off at a single draught, unmixed with water.

He then asked some further question, which I could not hear, manifesting, as it appeared, considerable excitement of mind. In answering him, Matthew glanced his eyes upward, as if indicating some room in the house. The young man then retired, hurriedly, through the sitting-room.

"What's the matter with Willy Hammond to-night?" asked some one of the bar-keeper. "Who's he after in such a hurry?"

"He wants to see Judge Lyman," replied Matthew.

"Oh!"

"I guess they're after no good," was remarked.

"Not much, I'm afraid."

Two young men, well dressed, and with faces marked by intelligence, came in at the moment, drank at the bar, chatted a little while familiarly with the barkeeper, and then quietly disappeared through the door leading into the sitting-room. I met the eyes of the man with whom I had talked during the afternoon, and his knowing wink brought to mind his suggestion, that in one of the upper rooms gambling went on nightly, and that some of the most promising young men of the town had been drawn, through the bar attraction, into this vortex of ruin. I felt a shudder creeping along my nerves.

The conversation that now went on among the company was of such an obscene and profane character that, in disgust, I went out. The night was clear, the air soft, and the moon shining down brightly. I walked for some time in the porch, musing on what I had seen and heard; while a constant stream of visitors came pouring into the bar-room. Only a few of these remained. The larger portion went in quickly, took their glass, and then left, as if to avoid observation as much as possible.

Soon after I commenced walking in the porch, I noticed an elderly lady go slowly by, who, in passing, slightly paused, and evidently tried to look through the bar-room door. The pause was but for an instant. In less than ten minutes she came back, again stopped—this time longer—and again moved off slowly, until she passed out of sight. I was yet thinking about her, when, on lifting my eyes from the ground, she was advancing along the road, but a few rods distant. I almost started at seeing her, for there no longer remained a doubt on my mind, that she was some trembling, heart-sick mother, in search of an erring son, whose feet were in dangerous paths. Seeing me, she kept on, though lingeringly. She went but a short distance before returning; and this time, she moved in closer to the house, and reached a position that enabled her eyes to range through a large portion of the bar-room. A nearer in-spection appeared to satisfy her. She retired with quicker steps; and did not again return during the evening.

Ah! what a commentary upon the uses of
13

an attractive tavern was here! My heart ached, as I thought of all that unknown mother had suffered; and, was doomed to suffer. I could not shut out the image of her drooping form as I lay upon my pillow that night; she even haunted me in my dreams.

NIGHT THE SIXTH.

MORE CONSEQUENCES.

THE landlord did not make his appearance on the next morning until nearly ten o'clock; and then he looked like a man who had been on a debauch. It was eleven before Harvey Green came down. Nothing about him indicated the smallest deviation from the most orderly habit. Clean shaved, with fresh linen, and a face, every line of which was smoothed into calmness, he looked as if he had slept soundly on a quiet conscience, and now hailed the new day with a tranquil spirit.

The first act of Slade was to go behind the bar and take a stiff glass of brandy and water; the first act of Green, to order beefsteak and coffee for his breakfast. I noticed the meeting between the two men, on the appearance of

Green. There was a slight reserve on the part of Green, and an uneasy embarrassment on the part of Slade. Not even the ghost of a smile was visible in either countenance. They spoke a few words together, and then separated as if from a sphere of mutual repulsion. I did not observe them again in company during the day.

"There's trouble over at the mill," was remarked by a gentleman with whom I had some business transactions in the afternoon. He spoke to a person who sat in his office.

"Ah! what's the matter?" said the other.

"All the hands were discharged at noon, and the mill shut down."

"How comes that?"

"They've been losing money from the start."

"Rather bad practice, I should say."

"It involves some bad practices, no doubt."

"On Willy's part?"

"Yes. He is reported to have squandered the means placed in his hands, after a shameless fashion."

"Is the loss heavy?"

"So it is said."

"How much?"

"Reaching to thirty or forty thousand dollars. But this is rumor, and, of course, an exaggeration."

"Of course. No such loss as that could have been made. But what was done with the money? How could Willy have spent it. He dashes about a great deal; buys fast horses, drinks rather freely, and all that; but thirty or forty thousand dollars couldn't escape in this way."

At the moment a swift trotting horse, bearing a light sulky and a man, went by.

"There goes young Hammond's three hundred dollar animal," said the last speaker.

"It was Willy Hammond's yesterday. But there has been a change of ownership since then; I happen to know."

"Indeed."

"Yes. The man Green, who has been loaf-

ing about Cedarville for the last few years—
after no good, I can well believe—came into
possession to-day."

"Ah! Willy must be very fickle-minded.
Does the possession of a coveted object so soon
bring satiety?"

"There is something not clearly understood
about the transaction. I saw Mr. Hammond
during the forenoon, and he looked terribly
distressed."

"The embarrassed condition of things at the
mill readily accounts for this."

"True; but I think there are causes of trouble beyond the mere embarrassments."

"The dissolute, spendthrift habits of his
son," was suggested. "These are sufficient to
weigh down the father's spirits,—to bow him
to the very dust."

"To speak out plainly," said the other, "I
am afraid that the young man adds another
vice to that of drinking and idleness."

"What?"

"Gaming."

"No!"

"There is little doubt of it in my mind. And it is further my opinion, that his fine horse, for which he paid three hundred dollars only a few days ago, has passed into the hands of this man Green, in payment of a debt contracted at the gaming table."

"You shock me. Surely, there can be no grounds for such a belief."

"I have, I am sorry to say, the gravest reasons for what I allege. That Green is a professional gambler, who was attracted here by the excellent company that assembled at the 'Sickle and Sheaf' in the beginning of the lazy miller's pauper-making experiment, I do not in the least question. Grant this, and take into account the fact that young Hammond has been much in his company, and you have sufficient cause for the most disastrous effects."

"If this be really so," observed the gentleman, over whose face a shadow of concern darkened, then Willy Hammond may not be his only victim."

"And is not, you may rest assured. If rumor be true, other of our promising young men are being drawn into the whirling circles that narrow toward a vortex of ruin."

In corroboration of this, I mentioned the conversation I had held with one of the frequenters of Slade's bar-room, on this very subject; and also what I had myself observed on the previous evening.

The man, who had until now been sitting quietly in a chair, started up, exclaiming as he did so—

"Merciful heaven! I never dreamed of this! Whose sons are safe?"

"No man's," was the answer of the gentleman in whose office we were sitting—"No man's—while there are such open doors to ruin as you may find at the 'Sickle and Sheaf.' Did not you vote the anti-temperance ticket at the last election?"

"I did," was the answer; "and from principle."

"On what were your principles based?" was inquired.

"On the broad foundations of civil liberty."

"The liberty to do good or evil, just as the individual may choose?"

"I would not like to say that. There are certain evils against which there can be no legislation that would not do harm. No civil power in this country has the right to say what a citizen shall eat or drink."

" But may not the people, in any community, pass laws, through their delegated law-makers, restraining evil-minded persons from injuring the common good?"

"Oh, certainly—certainly."

"And are you prepared to affirm, that a drinking-shop, where young men are corrupted —aye, destroyed, body and soul — does not work an injury to the common good?"

"Ah! but there must be houses of public entertainment."

"No one denies this. But can that be a really Christian community which provides for the moral debasement of strangers, at the same time that it entertains them? Is it necessary that, in giving rest and entertainment to the traveler, we also lead him into temptation?"

"Yes—but—but—it is going too far to legislate on wha we are to eat and drink. It is opening too wide a door for fanatical oppression. We must inculcate temperance as a right principle. We must teach our children the evils of intemperance, and send them out into the world as practical teachers of order, virtue, and sobriety. If we do this, the reform becomes radical, and in a few years there will be no bar-rooms, for none will crave the fiery poison."

"Of little value, my friend, will be, in far too many cases, your precepts, if temptation invites our sons at almost every step of their way through life. Thousands have fallen, and thousands are now tottering, soon to fall. Your sons are not safe; nor are mine. We cannot tell the day nor the hour when they may weakly yield to the solicitation of some companion, and enter the wide open door of ruin. And are we wise and good citizens to commission men to do the evil work of enticement? To encourage them to get gain in corrupting and destroying our children? To hesitate over some vague ideal of human liberty when the sword is among us, slaying our best and dearest? Sir! while you hold back from the work of staying the flood that is desolating our fairest homes, the black waters are approaching your own doors."

There was a startling emphasis in the tones with which this last sentence was uttered; and I did not wonder at the look of anxious alarm that it called to the face of him whose fears is was meant to excite.

"What do you mean, sir?" was inquired.

"Simply, that your sons are in equal danger with others."

"And is that all?"

"They have been seen, of late, in the bar-room of the 'Sickle and Sheaf.'"

"Who says so?"

"Twice within a week I have seen them going in there," was answered

"Good heavens! No!"

"It is true, my friend. But who is safe? If we dig pits, and conceal them from view, what marvel if our own children fall therein?"

"My sons going to a tavern?" The man seemed utterly confounded. "How *can* I believe it? You must be in error, sir."

"No. What I tell you is the simple truth. And if they go there——"

The man paused not to hear the conclusion of the sentence, but went hastily from the office.

"We are beginning to reap as we have

sown," remarked the gentleman, turning to me as his agitated friend left the office. "As I told them in the commencement it would be, so it is happening. The want of a good tavern in Cedarville was over and over again alleged as one of the chief causes of our want of thrift, and when Slade opened the 'Sickle and Sheaf,' the man was almost glorified. The gentleman who has just left us failed not in laudation of the enterprising landlord; the more particularly as the building of the new tavern advanced the price of ground on the street, and made him a few hundred dollars richer. Really, for a time, one might have thought, from the way people went on, that Simon Slade was going to make every man's fortune in Cedarville. But all that has been gained by a small advance in property, is as a grain of sand to a mountain, compared with the fearful demoralization that has followed."

I readily assented to this, for I had myself seen enough to justify the conclusion.

As I sat in the bar-room of the " Sickle and

Sheaf" that evening, I noticed, soon after the lamps were lighted, the gentleman referred to in the above conversation, whose sons were represented as visitors to the bar, come in quietly, and look anxiously about the room. He spoke to no one, and, after satisfying himself that those he sought were not there, went out.

"What sent him here, I wonder?" muttered Slade, speaking partly to himself, and partly aside to Matthew, the bar-keeper.

"After the boys, I suppose," was answered.

"I guess the boys are old enough to take care of themselves."

"They ought to be," returned Matthew.

"And are," said Slade. "Have they been here this evening?"

"No, not yet."

While they yet talked together, two young men whom I had seen on the night before, and noticed particularly as showing signs of intelligence and respectability beyond the ordinary visitors at a bar-room, came in.

"John," I heard Slade say, in a low, confidential voice, to one of them, "your old man was here just now."

"No!" The young man looked startled—almost confounded.

"It's a fact. So you'd better keep shady."

"What did he want!"

"I don't know."

"What did he say?"

"Nothing. He just came in, looked around, and then went out."

"His face was as dark as a thunder-cloud," remarked Matthew.

"Is No. 4 vacant?" inquired one of the young men.

"Yes."

"Send us up a bottle of wine and some cigars. And when Bill Harding and Harry Lee come in, tell them where they can find us."

"All right," said Matthew. "And now, take a friend's advice, and make yourself scarce."

The young men left the room hastily. Scarcely had they departed, ere I saw the same gentleman come in, whose anxious face had, a little while before, thrown its shadow over the apartment. He was the father in search of his sons. Again he glanced around, nervously; and this time appeared to be disappointed. As he entered, Slade went out.

"Have John and Wilson been here this evening?" he asked, coming up to the bar and addressing Matthew.

"They are not here," replied Matthew, evasively.

"But haven't they been here?"

"They *may* have been here; I only came in from my supper a little while ago."

"I thought I saw them entering, only a moment or two ago."

"They're not here, sir." Matthew shook his head and spoke firmly.

"Where is Mr. Slade?"

"In the house, somewhere."

"I wish you would ask him to step here."

Matthew went out, but in a little while came back with word that the landlord was not to be found.

"You are sure the boys are not here?" said the man, with a doubting, dissatisfied manner.

"See for yourself, Mr. Harrison!"

"Perhaps they are in the parlor?"

"Step in, sir," coolly returned Matthew. The man went through the door into the sitting-room, but came back immediately.

"Not there?" said Matthew. The man shook his head. "I don't think you will find them about here," added the bar-keeper.

Mr. Harrison—this was the name by which Matthew had addressed him—stood musing and irresolute for some minutes. He could not be mistaken about the entrance of his sons, and yet they were not there. His manner was much perplexed. At length he took a seat, in a far corner of the bar-room, somewhat beyond the line of observation, evidently with the purpose of waiting to see if those he sought would come in. He had not been there long, before two young men entered, whose appearance at once excited his interest. They went up to the bar and called for liquor. As Matthew set the decanter before them, he leaned over the counter, and said something in a whisper.

"Where?" was instantly ejaculated, in surprise, and both of the young men glanced uneasily about the room. They met the eyes of Mr. Harrison fixed intently upon them. I do not think, from the way they swallowed their brandy and water, that it was enjoyed very much.

"What the deuce is he doing here?" I heard one of them say in a low voice.

"After the boys, of course."

"Have they come yet?"

Matthew winked as he answered, "All safe."

"In No. 4?"

"Yes. And the wine and cigars all waiting for you."

" Good."

" You'd better not go through the parlor. Their old man's not at all satisfied. He half suspects they're in the house. Better go off down the street, and come back and enter through the passage."

The young men, acting on this hint, at once retired, the eyes of Harrison following them out.

For nearly an hour Mr. Harrison kept his position, a close observer of all that transpired. I am very much in error, if, before leaving that sink of iniquity, he was not fully satisfied as to the propriety of legislating on the liquor question. Nay, I incline to the opinion, that, if the power of suppression had rested in his hands, there would not have been, in the whole State, at the expiration of an hour, a single dram-selling establishment. The goring of his ox had opened his eyes to the true merits of the question. While he was yet in the bar-room, young Hammond made his appearance. His look was wild and excited. First he called for brandy, and drank with the eagerness of a man long athirst.

"Where is Green?" I heard him inquire, as he set his glass upon the counter.

"Haven't seen any thing of him since supper," was answered by Matthew.

"Is he in his room?"

"I think it probable."

"Has Judge Lyman been about here to-night?"

"Yes. He spouted here for half an hour against the temperance party, as usual, and then"—Matthew tossed his head toward the door leading to the sitting-room.

Hammond was moving toward this door, when, in glancing around the room, he encountered the fixed gaze of Mr. Harrison—a gaze that instantly checked his progress. Returning to the bar, and leaning over the counter, he said to Matthew:

"What has sent him here?"

Matthew winked knowingly.

"After the boys?" inquired Hammond.

"Yes."

"Where are they?"

"Up-stairs."

"Does he suspect this?"

"I can't tell. If he doesn't think them here now, he is looking for them to come in."

"Do they know he is after them?"

"O yes."

"All safe then?"

"As an iron chest. If you want to see them, just rap at No. 4."

Hammond stood for some minutes leaning on the bar, and then, not once again looking toward that part of the room where Mr. Harrison was seated, passed out through the door leading to the street. Soon afterward Mr. Harrison departed.

Disgusted, as on the night before, with the unceasing flow of vile, obscene, and profane language, I left my place of observation in the bar-room and sought the open air. The sky was unobscured by a single cloud, and the moon, almost at the full, shone abroad with more than common brightness. I had not been sitting long in the porch, when the same lady, whose movements had attracted my attention, came in sight, walking very slowly—the deliberate pace assumed, evidently, for the purpose of better observation. On coming opposite the tavern, she slightly paused, as on the evening before, and then kept on, passing down the street, until she was beyond observation.

"Poor mother!" I was still repeating to myself, when her form again met my eyes. Slowly she advanced, and now came in nearer to the house. The interest excited in my mind was so strong, that I could not repress the desire I felt to address her, and so stepped from the shadow of the porch. She seemed startled, and retreated backward several paces.

"Are you in search of any one?" I inquired, respectfully.

The woman now stood in a position that let the moon shine full upon her face, revealing every feature. She was far past the meridian of life; and there were lines of suffering and sorrow on her fine countenance. I saw that her lips moved, but it was some time before I distinguished the words.

"Have you seen my son to-night? They say he comes here."

The manner in which this was said caused a cold thrill to run over me. I perceived that the woman's mind wandered. I answered:

"No, ma'am; I haven't seen any thing of him."

My tone of voice seemed to inspire her with confidence, for she came up close to me, and bent her face toward mine.

"It's a dreadful place," she whispered, huskily. "And they say he comes here. Poor boy! He isn't what he used to be."

"It is a very bad place," said I. "Come"— and I moved a step or two in the direction from which I had seen her approaching—"come, you'd better go away as quickly as possible."

"But if he's here," she answered, not moving from where she stood, " I might save him, you know."

" I am sure you won't find him, ma'am," I urged. " Perhaps he is home, now."

"Oh, no! no!" And she shook her head mournfully. "He never comes home until long after midnight. I wish I could see inside of the bar-room. I'm sure he must be there."

" If you will tell me his name, I will go in and search for him."

After a moment of hesitation, she answered:

" His name is Willy Hammond."

How the name, uttered so sadly, and yet with such moving tenderness by the mother's lips, caused me to start—almost to tremble.

" If he is in the house, ma'am," said I, firmly, " I will see him for you." And I left her and went into the bar.

"In what room do you think I will find young Hammond?" I asked of the bar-keeper.

He looked at me curiously, but did not answer. The question had come upon him unanticipated.

"In Harvey Green's room?" I pursued.

"I don't know, I am sure. He isn't in the house to my knowledge. I saw him go out about half an hour since."

"Green's room is No.——?"

"Eleven," he answered:

"In the front part of the house?"

"Yes."

I asked no further question, but went to No. 11, and tapped on the door. But no one answered the summons. I listened, but could not distinguish the slightest sound within. Again I knocked; but louder. If my ears did not deceive me, the chink of coin was heard. Still there was neither voice nor movement.

I was disappointed. That the room had inmates, I felt sure. Remembering, now, what I had heard about light being seen in this room through a rent in the curtain, I went down-stairs, and out into the street. A short distance beyond the house, I saw, dimly, the woman's form. She had only just passed in her movement to and fro. Glancing up at the window, which I now knew to be the one in Green's room, light through the torn curtain was plainly visible. Back into the house I went, and up to No. 11. This time I knocked imperatively; and this time made myself heard.

"What's wanted?" came from within. I knew the voice to be that of Harvey Green.

I only knocked louder. A hurried movement and the low murmur of voices was heard for some moments; then the door was unlocked and held partly open by Green, whose body so filled the narrow aperture that I could not look into the room. Seeing me, a dark scowl fell upon his countenance.

"What d'ye want?" he inquired, sharply.

"Is Mr. Hammond here? If so, he is wanted down-stairs."

"No, he's not," was the quick answer. "What sent you here for him, hey?"

"The fact that I expected to find him in your room," was the firm answer.

Green was about shutting the door in my face, when some one placed a hand on his shoulder, and said something to him that I could not hear.

"Who wants to see him?" he inquired of me.

Satisfied, now, that Hammond was in the room, I said, slightly elevating my voice:

"His mother."

The words were an "open sesame" to the room. The door was suddenly jerked open, and with a blanching face, the young man confronted me.

"Who says my mother is down-stairs?" he demanded.

"I come from her in search of you," I said.

"You will find her in the road, walking up and down in front of the tavern."

Almost with a bound he swept by me, and descended the stairway at two or three long strides. As the door swung open, I saw, besides Green and Hammond, the landlord and Judge Lyman. It needed not the loose cards on the table near which the latter were sitting to tell me of their business in that room.

As quickly as seemed decorous, I followed Hammond. On the porch I met him, coming in from the road.

"You have deceived me, sir," said he, sternly —almost menacingly.

"No, sir!" I replied. "What I told you was but too true. Look! There she is now."

The young man sprung around, and stood before the woman, a few paces distant.

"Mother! oh, mother! what *has* brought you here?" he exclaimed, in an undertone, as he caught her arm, and moved away. He spoke—not roughly, nor angrily—but with respect—half reproachfulness—and an unmistakable tenderness.

"Oh, Willy! Willy!" I heard her answer. "Somebody said you came here at night, and I couldn't rest. Oh, dear! They'll murder you! I know they will. Don't, oh!——"

My ears took in the sense no further, though her pleading voice still reached my ears. A few moments, and they were out of sight.

Nearly two hours afterward, as I was ascending to my chamber, a man brushed quickly by me. I glanced after him, and recognized the person of young Hammond. He was going to the room of Harvey Green!

NIGHT THE SEVENTH.

SOWING THE WIND.

THE state of affairs in Cedarville, it was plain, from the partial glimpses I had received, was rather desperate. Desperate, I mean, as regarded the various parties brought before my observation. An eating cancer was on the community, and so far as the eye could mark its destructive progress, the ravages were fearful. That its roots were striking deep, and penetrating, concealed from view, in many unsuspected directions, there could be no doubt. What appeared on the surface was but a milder form of the disease, compared with its hidden, more vital, and more dangerous advances.

I could not but feel a strong interest in some of these parties. The case of young Hammond had, from the first, awakened concern; and now

a new element was added in the unlooked-for
appearance of his mother on the stage, in a
state that seemed one of partial derangement.
The gentleman at whose office I met Mr. Harrison on the day before—the reader will remember Mr. H. as having come to the "Sickle
and Sheaf" in search of his sons—was thoroughly conversant with the affairs of the village, and I called upon him early in the day in
order to make some inquiries about Mrs. Hammond. My first question, as to whether he
knew the lady, was answered by the remark:

"Oh, yes. She is one of my earliest friends."

The allusion to her did not seem to awaken
agreeable states of mind. A slight shade obscured his face, and I noticed that he sighed
involuntarily.

"Is Willy her only child?"

"Her only living child. She had four; another son, and two daughters; but she lost all
but Willy when they were quite young. And,"
he added, after a pause—"it would have been

better for her, and for Willy too, if he had gone to a better land with them."

" His course of life must be to her a terrible affliction," said I.

"It is destroying her reason," he replied, with emphasis. " He was her idol. No mother ever loved a son with more self-devotion than Mrs. Hammond loved her beautiful, fine-spirited, intelligent, affectionate boy. To say that she was proud of him, is but a tame expression. Intense love—almost idolatry—was the strong passion of her heart. How tender, how watchful was her love! Except when at school, he was scarcely ever separated from her. In order to keep him by her side, she gave up her thoughts to the suggestion and maturing of plans for keeping his mind active and interested in her society—and her success was perfect. Up to the age of sixteen or seventeen, I do not think he had a desire for other companionship than that of his mother. But this, you know, could not last. The boy's maturing thought must go beyond the home and social circle. The great world, that he was soon to enter, was before him; and through loopholes that opened here and there he obtained partial glimpses of what was beyond. To step forth into this world, where he was soon to be a busy actor and worker, and to step forth alone, next came in the natural order of progress. How his mother trembled with anxiety, as she saw him leave her side! Of the dangers that would surround his path, she knew too well; and these were magnified by her fears—at least so I often said to her. Alas! how far the sad reality has outrun her most fearful anticipations.

"When Willy was eighteen—he was then reading law—I think I never saw a young man of fairer promise. As I have often heard it remarked of him, he did not appear to have a single fault. But he had a dangerous gift— rare conversational powers, united with great urbanity of manner. Every one who made his acquaintance became charmed with his society;

15

and he soon found himself surrounded by a circle of young men, some of whom were not the best companions he might have chosen. Still, his own pure instincts and honorable principles were his safeguard; and I never have believed that any social allurements would have drawn him away from the right path, if this accursed tavern had not been opened by Slade."

"There was a tavern here before the 'Sickle and Sheaf' was opened?" said I.

"Oh, yes. But it was badly kept, and the bar-room visitors were of the lowest class. No respectable young man in Cedarville would have been seen there. It offered no temptations to one moving in Willy's circle. But the opening of the 'Sickle and Sheaf' formed a new era. Judge Hammond—himself not the purest man in the world, I'm afraid—gave his countenance to the establishment, and talked of Simon Slade as an enterprising man who ought to be encouraged. Judge Lyman and other men of position in Cedarville followed his bad example; and the bar-room of the 'Sickle and Sheaf' was at once voted respectable. At all times of the day and evening you could see the flower of our young men going in and out, sitting in front of the bar-room, or talking hand and glove with the landlord, who, from a worthy miller, regarded as well enough in his place, was suddenly elevated into a man of importance, whom the best in the village were delighted to honor.

"In the beginning, Willy went with the tide, and, in an incredibly short period, was acquiring a fondness for drink that startled and alarmed his friends. In going in through Slade's open door, he entered the downward way, and has been moving onward with fleet footsteps ever since. The fiery poison inflamed his mind, at the same time that it dimmed his noble perceptions. Fondness for mere pleasure followed, and this led him into various sensual indulgences, and exciting modes of passing the

time. Every one liked him—he was so free, so
companionable, and so generous—and almost
every one encouraged, rather than repressed,
his dangerous proclivities. Even his father,
for a time, treated the matter lightly, as only
the first flush of young life. 'I commenced
sowing my wild oats at quite as early an age,'
I have heard him say. 'He'll cool off, and do
well enough. Never fear.' But his mother
was in a state of painful alarm from the beginning. Her truer instincts, made doubly
acute by her yearning love, perceived the im-
minent danger, and in all possible ways did she
seek to lure him from the path in which he was
moving at so rapid a pace. Willy was always
very much attached to his mother, and her influence over him was strong; but in this case
he regarded her fears as chimerical. The way
in which he walked was, to him, so pleasant,
and the companions of his journey so delight-
ful, that he could not believe in the prophesied
evil; and when his mother talked to him in

her warning voice, and with a sad countenance, he smiled at her concern, and made light of her fears.

"And so it went on, month after month, and year after year, until the young man's sad declensions were the town talk. In order to throw his mind into a new channel—to awaken, if possible, a new and better interest in life—his father ventured upon the doubtful experiment we spoke of yesterday: that of placing capital in his hands, and making him an equal partner in the business of distilling and cotton-spinning. The disastrous—I might say disgraceful—result you know. The young man squandered his own capital, and heavily embarrassed his father.

"The effect of all this upon Mrs. Hammond has been painful in the extreme. We can only dimly imagine the terrible suffering through which she has passed. Her present aberration was first visible after a long period of sleeplessness, occasioned by distress of mind. During

the whole of two weeks, I am told, she did not
close her eyes; the most of that time walking
the floor of her chamber, and weeping. Powerful anodynes, frequently repeated, at length
brought relief. But, when she awoke from
a prolonged period of unconsciousness, the
brightness of her reason was gone. Since then,
she has never been clearly conscious of what
was passing around her, and well for her, I
have sometimes thought it was, for even ob-
scurity of intellect is a blessing in her case.
Ah, me! I always get the heart-ache, when I
think of her."

"Did not this event startle the young man
from his fatal dream, if I may so call his mad
infatuation?" I asked.

"No. He loved his mother, and was deeply
afflicted by the calamity; but it seemed as if
he could not stop. Some terrible necessity appeared to be impelling him onward. If he
formed good resolutions—and I doubt not that
he did—they were blown away like threads of

gossamer, the moment he came within the sphere of old associations. His way to the mill was by the 'Sickle and Sheaf;' and it was not easy for him to pass there without being drawn into the bar, either by his own desire for drink, or through the invitation of some pleasant companion, who was lounging in front of the tavern."

"There may have been something even more impelling than his love of drink," said I.

"What?"

I related, briefly, the occurrences of the preceding night.

"I feared—nay, I was certain—that he was in the toils of this man! And yet your confirmation of the fact startles and confounds me," said he, moving about his office in a disturbed manner. "If my mind has questioned and doubted in regard to young Hammond, it questions and doubts no longer. The word 'mystery' is not now written over the door of his habitation. Great Father! and is it thus

that our young men are led into temptation?
Thus that their ruin is premeditated, secured?
Thus that the fowler is permitted to spread his
net in the open day, and the destroyer licensed
to work ruin in darkness? It is awful to con-
template!"

The man was strongly excited.

"Thus it is," he continued; "and we who
see the whole extent, origin, and downward
rushing force of a widely sweeping desolation,
lift our voices of warning almost in vain. Men
who have every thing at stake—sons to be corrupted, and daughters to become the wives of
young men exposed to corrupting influences—
stand aloof, questioning and doubting as to the
expediency of protecting the innocent from the
wolfish designs of bad men; who, to compass
their own selfish ends, would destroy them
body and soul. We are called fanatics, ultra-
ists, designing, and all that, because we ask our
law-makers to stay the fiery ruin. Oh, no! we
must not touch the traffic. All the dearest and

best interests of society may suffer; but the rum-seller must be protected. He must be allowed to get gain, if the jails and poor-houses are filled, and the graveyards made fat with the bodies of young men stricken down in the flower of their years, and of wives and mothers who have died of broken hearts. Reform, we are told, must commence at home. We must rear temperate children, and then we shall have temperate men. That when there are none to desire liquor, the rum-seller's traffic will cease. And all the while society's true benefactors are engaged in doing this, the weak, the unsuspecting, and the erring must be left an easy prey, even if the work requires for its accomplishment a hundred years. Sir! a human soul destroyed through the rum-seller's infernal agency, is a sacrifice priceless in value. No considerations of worldly gain can, for an instant, be placed in comparison therewith. And yet souls are destroyed by thousands every year; and they will fall by tens of thousands

ere society awakens from its fatal indifference, and lays its strong hand of power on
the corrupt men who are scattering disease, ruin, and death, broadcast over the
land!

"I always get warm on this subject," he
added, repressing his enthusiasm. "And
who that observes and reflects can help growing excited! The evil is appalling; and the
indifference of the community one of the
strangest facts of the day."

While he was yet speaking, the elder Mr.
Hammond came in. He looked wretched. The
redness and humidity of his eyes showed want
of sleep, and the relaxed muscles of his face
exhaustion from weariness and suffering. He
drew the person with whom I had been talking aside, and continued in earnest conversation with him for many minutes—often gesticu-
lating violently. I could see his face, though
I heard nothing of what he said. The play of
his features was painful to look upon, for every

changing muscle showed a new phase of mental suffering.

"Try and see him, will you not?" he said, as he turned, at length, to leave the office.

"I will go there immediately," was answered.

"Bring him home, if possible."

"My very best efforts shall be made."

Judge Hammond bowed, and went out hurriedly.

"Do you know the number of the room occupied by the man Green?" asked the gentleman, as soon as his visitor had retired.

"Yes. It is No. 11."

"Willy has not been home since last night. His father, at this late day, suspects Green to be a gambler. The truth flashed upon him only yesterday; and this, added to his other sources of trouble, is driving him, so he says, almost mad. As a friend, he wishes me to go to the 'Sickle and Sheaf,' and try and find Willy. Have you seen anything of him this morning?"

I answered in the negative.

"Nor of Green?"

"No."

"Was Slade about when you left the tavern?"

"I saw nothing of him."

"What Judge Hammond fears may be all too true—that, in the present condition of Willy's affairs, which have reached the point of disaster, his tempter means to secure the largest possible share of property yet in his power to pledge or transfer,—to squeeze from his victim the last drop of blood that remains, and then fling him, ruthlessly, from his hands."

"The young man must have been rendered almost desperate, or he would never have returned, as he did, last night. Did you mention this to his father?"

"No. It would have distressed him the more, without effecting any good. He is wretched enough. But time passes, and none is to be lost now. Will you go with me?"

I walked to the tavern with him; and we went into the bar together. Two or three men were at the counter, drinking.

"Is Mr. Green about this morning?" was asked by the person who had come in search of young Hammond.

"Haven't seen anything of him."

"Is he in his room?"

"I don't know."

"Will you ascertain for me?"

"Certainly. Frank,"—and he spoke to the landlord's son, who was lounging on a settee, —"I wish you would see if Mr. Green is in his room."

"Go and see yourself. I'm not your waiter," was growled back, in an ill-natured voice.

"In a moment I'll ascertain for you," said Matthew, politely.

After waiting on some new customers, who were just entering, Matthew went up-stairs to obtain the desired information. As he left the bar-room, Frank got up and went behind the counter, where he mixed himself a glass of liquor, and drank it off, evidently with real enjoyment.

"Rather a dangerous business for one so young as you are," remarked the gentleman with whom I had come, as Frank stepped out of the bar, and passed near where we were standing. The only answer to this was an ill-natured frown, and an expression of face which said almost as plainly as words, "It's none of your business."

"Not there," said Matthew, now coming in.

"Are you certain?"

"Yes, sir."

But there was a certain involuntary hesitation in the bar-keeper's manner, which led to a suspicion that his answer was not in accordance with the truth. We walked out together, conferring on the subject, and both concluded that his word was not to be relied upon.

"What is to be done?" was asked.

"Go to Green's room," I replied, "and knock

at the door. If he is there, he may answer, not suspecting your errand."

"Show me the room."

I went up with him, and pointed out No. 11. He knocked lightly, but there came no sound from within. He repeated the knock; all was silent. Again and again he knocked, but there came back only a hollow reverberation.

"There's no one there," said he, returning to where I stood, and we walked down-stairs together. On the landing, as we reached the lower passage, we met Mrs. Slade. I had not, during this visit at Cedarville, stood face to face with her before. Oh! what a wreck she presented, with her pale, shrunken countenance, hollow, lustreless eyes, and bent, feeble body. I almost shuddered as I looked at her. What a haunting and sternly rebuking spectre she must have moved, daily, before the eyes of her husband.

"Have you noticed Mr. Green about this morning?" I asked.

"He hasn't come down from his room yet," she replied.

"Are you certain?" said my companion. "I knocked several times at the door just now, but received no answer."

"What do you want with him?" asked Mrs. Slade, fixing her eyes upon us.

"We are in search of Willy Hammond; and it has been suggested that he is with Green."

"Knock twice lightly, and then three times more firmly," said Mrs. Slade; and as she spoke, she glided past us with noiseless tread.

"Shall we go up together?"

I did not object; for, although I had no delegated right of intrusion, my feelings were so much excited in the case, that I went forward, scarcely reflecting on the propriety of so doing.

The signal knock found instant answer. The door was softly opened, and the unshaven face of Simon Slade presented itself.

"Mr. Jacobs!" he said, with surprise in his tones. "Do you wish to see me!"

"No, sir! I wish to see Mr. Green," and with a quick, firm pressure against the door, he pushed it wide open. The same party was there that I had seen on the night before,— Green, young Hammond, Judge Lyman, and Slade. On the table at which the three former were sitting, were cards, slips of paper, an ink-stand and pens, and a pile of bank-notes. On a side-table, or, rather, butler's tray, were bottles, decanters, and glasses.

"Judge Lyman! Is it possible?" exclaimed Mr. Jacobs, the name of my companion; "I did not expect to find you hear."

Green instantly swept his hands over the table to secure the money and bills it contained; but, ere he had accomplished his purpose, young Hammond grappled three or four narrow strips of paper, and hastily tore them into shreds.

"You're a cheating scoundrel!" cried Green,

16

fiercely, thrusting his hand into his bosom as if
to draw from thence a weapon ; but the words
were scarcely uttered, ere Hammond sprung
upon him with the fierceness of a tiger, bearing
him down upon the floor. Both hands were
already about the gambler's neck, and, ere the
bewildered spectators could interfere, and drag
him off, Green was purple in the face, and
nearly strangled.

"Call me a cheating scoundrel!" said Hammond, foaming at the mouth, as he spoke,—
"Me! whom you have followed like a thirsty
bloodhound. Me! whom you have robbed,
and cheated, and debased from the beginning!
Oh! for a pistol to rid the earth of the black-
est-hearted villain that walks its surface. Let
me go, gentlemen! I have nothing left in the
world to care for,—there is no consequence I
fear. Let me do society one good service before I die!"

And, with one vigorous effort, he swept himself clear of the hands that were pinioning him,

"WILLY HAMMOND MURDERED BY THE GAMBLER, HARVEY GREEN."

and sprung again upon the gambler with the fierce energy of a savage beast. By this time, Green had got his knife free from its sheath, and, as Hammond was closing upon him in his blind rage, plunged it into his side. Quick almost as lightning, the knife was withdrawn, and two more stabs inflicted ere we could seize and disarm the murderer. As we did so, Willy Hammond fell over with a deep groan, the blood flowing from his side.

In the terror and excitement that followed, Green rushed from the room. The doctor, who was instantly summoned, after carefully examining the wound, and the condition of the unhappy young man, gave it as his opinion that he was fatally injured.

Oh! the anguish of the father, who had quickly heard of the dreadful occurrence, when this announcement was made. I never saw such fearful agony in any human countenance. The calmest of all the anxious group was Willy himself. On his father's

face his eyes were fixed as if by a kind of fas-
cination.

"Are you in much pain, my poor boy?"
sobbed the old man, stooping over him, until
his long white hair mingled with the damp
locks of the sufferer.

"Not much, father," was the whispered reply. "Don't speak of this to mother, yet. I'm
afraid it will kill her."

What could the father answer? Nothing!
And he was silent.

"Does she know of it?" A shadow went
over his face.

Mr. Hammond shook his head.

Yet, even as he spoke, a wild cry of distress
was heard below. Some indiscreet person had
borne to the ears of the mother the fearful news
about her son, and she had come wildly flying
toward the tavern, and was just entering.

"It is my poor mother," said Willy, a flush
coming into his pale face. "Who could have
told her of this?"

Mr. Hammond started for the door, but ere he had reached it, the distracted mother entered.

"Oh! Willy, my boy! my boy!" she exclaimed, in tones of anguish that made the heart shudder. And she crouched down on the floor, the moment she reached the bed whereon he lay, and pressed her lips—oh, so tenderly and lovingly!—to his.

"Dear mother! Sweet mother! Best of mothers!" He even smiled as he said this; and, into the face that now bent over him, looked up with glances of unutterable fondness.

"Oh, Willy! Willy! Willy! my son, my son!" And again her lips were laid closely to his.

Mr. Hammond now interfered, and endeavored to remove his wife, fearing for the consequence upon his son.

"Don't father!" said Willy; "let her remain. I am not excited nor disturbed. I am glad that she is here, now. It will be best for us both."

"You must not excite him, dear," said Mr. Hammond—"he is very weak."

"I'll not excite him," answered the mother. "I'll not speak a word. There, love"—and she laid her fingers softly upon the lips of her son —"don't speak a single word."

For only a few moments did she sit with the quiet formality of a nurse, who feels how much depends on the repose of her patient. Then she began, weeping, moaning, and wringing her hands.

"Mother!" The feeble voice of Willy stilled, instantly, the tempest of feeling. "Mother, kiss me!"

She bent down and kissed him.

"Are you there, mother?" His eyes moved about, with a straining motion.

"Yes, love, here I am."

"I don't see you, mother. It's getting so dark. Oh, mother! mother!" he shouted sud-

denly, starting up and throwing himself for·
ward upon her bosom—"save me! save me!"

How quickly did the mother clasp her arms
around him—how eagerly did she strain him
to her bosom! The doctor, fearing the worst
consequences, now came forward, and endeav·
ored to release the arms of Mrs. Hammond, but
she resisted every attempt to do so.

"I will save you, my son," she murmured in
the ear of the young man. "Your mother
will protect you. Oh! if you had never left
her side, nothing on earth could have done you
harm."

"He is dead!" I heard the doctor whisper;
and a thrill of horror went through me. The
words reached the ears of Mr. Hammond, and
his groan was one of almost mortal agony.

"Who says he is dead?" came sharply from
the lips of the mother, as she pressed the form
of her child back upon the bed from which he
had sprung to her arms, and looked wildly
upon his face. One long scream of horror told

of her convictions, and she fell, lifeless, across the body of her dead son!

All in the room believed that Mrs. Hammond had only fainted. But the doctor's perplexed, troubled countenance, as he ordered her carried into another apartment, and the ghastliness of her face when it was upturned to the light, suggested to every one what proved to be true. Even to her obscured perceptions, the consciousness that her son was dead came with a terrible vividness—so terrible, that it extinguished her life.

Like fire among dry stubble ran the news of this fearful event through Cedarville. The whole town was wild with excitement. The prominent fact, that Willy Hammond had been murdered by Green, whose real profession was known by many, and now declared to all, was on every tongue; but a hundred different and exaggerated stories as to the cause and the particulars of the event were in circulation. By the time preparations to remove the dead

"ONE LONG SCREAM OF HORROR, AND SHE FELL, LIFELESS, ACROSS THE
BODY OF HER DEAD SON."

bodies of mother and son from the "Sickle and Sheaf" to the residence of Mr. Hammond were completed, hundreds of people, men, women, and children, were assembled around the tavern; and many voices were clamorous for Green; while some called out for Judge Lyman, whose name, it thus appeared, had become associated in the minds of the people with the murderous affair. The appearance, in the midst of this excitement, of the two dead bodies, borne forth on settees, did not tend to allay the feverish state of indignation that prevailed. From more than one voice, I heard the words, "Lynch the scoundrel!"

A part of the crowd followed the sad procession, while the greater portion, consisting of men, remained about the tavern. All bodies, no matter for what purpose assembled, quickly find leading spirits who, feeling the great moving impulse, give it voice and direction. It was so in this case. Intense indignation against Green was firing every bosom; and when a man

elevated himself a few feet above the agitated
mass of humanity, and cried out:

"The murderer must not escape!"

A wild responding shout, terrible in its
fierceness, made the air quiver.

"Let ten men be chosen to search the house
and premises," said the leading spirit.

"Ay! ay! Choose them! Name them!"
was quickly answered.

Ten men were called by name, who instantly
stepped in front of the crowd.

"Search everywhere; from garret to cellar;
from hayloft to dog-kennel. Everywhere!
everywhere!" cried the man.

And instantly the ten men entered the
house. For nearly a quarter of an hour, the
crowd waited with increasing signs of im-
patience. These delegates at length appeared,
with the announcement that Green was nowhere about the premises. It was received
with a groan.

"Let no man in Cedarville do a stroke of

work until the murderer is found," now shouted the individual who still occupied his elevated position.

"Agreed! agreed! No work in Cedarville until the murderer is found," rang out fiercely.

· "Let all who have horses, saddle and bridle them as quickly as possible, and assemble, mounted, at the Court House."

About fifty men left the crowd hastily.

"Let the crowd part in the centre, up and down the road, starting from a line in front of me."

This order was obeyed.

"Separate again, taking the centre of the road for a line."

Four distinct bodies of men stood now in front of the tavern.

"Now search for the murderer in every nook and corner, for a distance of three miles from this spot; each party keeping to its own section; the road being one dividing line, and a line through the centre of this tavern the other. The horsemen will pursue the wretch to a greater distance."

More than a hundred acquiescing voices responded to this, as the man sprung down from his elevation and mingled with the crowd, which began instantly to move away on its appointed mission.

As the hours went by, one, and another, and another, of the searching party returned to the village, wearied with their efforts, or confident that the murderer had made good his escape. The horsemen, too, began to come in, during the afternoon, and by sundown, the last of them, worn out and disappointed, made their appearance.

For hours after the exciting events of the forenoon, there were but few visitors at the "Sickle and Sheaf." Slade, who did not show himself among the crowd, came down soon after its dispersion. He had shaved and put on clean linen; but still bore many evidences of a night spent without sleep. His eyes were red and heavy and the eyelids swollen; while his skin was relaxed and colorless. As he descended the stairs, I was walking in the passage. He looked shy at me, and merely nodded. Guilt was written plainly on his countenance; and with it was blended anxiety and alarm. That he might be involved in trouble, he had reason to fear; for he was one of the party engaged in gambling in Green's room, as both Mr. Jacobs and I had witnessed.

"This is dreadful business," said he, as we met, face to face, half an hour afterward. He did not look me steadily in the eyes.

"It is horrible!" I answered. "To corrupt and ruin a young man, and then murder him! There are few deeds in the catalogue of crime blacker than this."

"It was done in the heat of passion," said the landlord, with something of apology in his manner. "Green never meant to kill him."

"In peaceful intercourse with his fellow-men, why did he carry a deadly weapon? There was murder in his heart, sir."

"That is speaking very strongly."

"Not stronger than facts will warrant," I replied. "That Green is a murderer in heart, it needed not this awful consummation to show. With a cool, deliberate purpose, he has sought, from the beginning, to destroy young Hammond."

"It is hardly fair," answered Slade, "in the present feverish excitement against Green, to assume such a questionable position. It may do him a great wrong."

"Did Willy Hammond speak only idle words, when he accused Green of having followed him like a thirsty bloodhound?—of having robbed, and cheated, and debased him from the beginning?"

"He was terribly excited at the moment."

"Yet," said I, "no ear that heard his words could for an instant doubt that they were truthful utterances, wrung from a maddened heart."

My earnest, positive manner had its effect upon Slade. He knew that what I asserted, the whole history of Green's intercourse with young Hammond would prove; and he had, moreover, the guilty consciousness of being a party to the young man's ruin. His eyes cowered beneath the steady gaze I fixed upon him. I thought of him as one implicated in the murder, and my thought must have been visible in my face.

"One murder will not justify another," said he.

"There is no justification for murder on any plea," was my response.

"And yet, if these infuriated men find Green, they will murder him."

"I hope not. Indignation at a horrible crime has fearfully excited the people. But I think their sense of justice is strong enough to prevent the consequences you apprehend."

"I would not like to be in Green's shoes," said the landlord, with an uneasy movement.

I looked him closely in the face. It was the punishment of the man's crime that seemed so fearful in his eyes; not the crime itself. Alas! how the corrupting traffic had debased him.

My words were so little relished by Slade, that he found some ready excuse to leave me. I saw but little more of him during the day.

As evening began to fall, the gambler's unsuccessful pursuers, one after another, found their way to the tavern, and by the time night had fairly closed in, the bar-room was crowded with excited and angry men, chafing over their disappointment, and loud in their threats of vengeance. That Green had made good his escape, was now the general belief; and the stronger this conviction became, the more steadily did the current of passion begin to set in a new direction. It had become known to every one that, besides Green and young Hammond, Judge Lyman and Slade were in

the room engaged in playing cards. The
merest suggestion as to the complicity of these
two men with Green in ruining Hammond, and
thus driving him mad, was enough to excite
strong feeling against them; and now that the
mob had been cheated of its victim, its pent-
up indignation sought eagerly some new channel.

"Where's Slade?" some one asked, in a loud
voice, from the centre of the crowded bar-room.
"Why does he keep himself out of sight?"

"Yes; where's the landlord?" half a dozen
voices responded.

"Did he go on the hunt?" some one inquired.

"No!" "No!" "No!" ran round the room.
"Not he."

"And yet, the murder was committed in his
own house, and before his own eyes!"

"Yes, before his own eyes!" repeated one
and another, indignantly.

"Where's Slade? Where's the landlord?

17

Has anybody seen him to-night? Matthew, where's Simon Slade?"

From lip to lip passed these interrogations; while the crowd of men became agitated, and swayed to and fro.

"I don't think he's home," answered the bar-keeper, in a hesitating manner, and with visible alarm.

"How long since he was here?"

"I haven't seen him for a couple of hours."

"That's a lie!" was sharply said.

"Who says it's a lie?" Matthew affected to be strongly indignant.

"I do!" And a rough, fierce-looking man confronted him.

"What right have you to say so?" asked Matthew, cooling off considerably.

"Because you lie!" said the man, boldly. "You've seen him within a less time than half an hour, and well you know it. Now, if you wish to keep yourself out of this trouble, answer truly. We are in no mood to deal with liars or equivocators. Where is Simon Slade?"

"I do not know," replied Matthew, firmly.

"Is he in the house?"

"He may be, or he may not be. I am just as ignorant of his exact whereabouts as you are."

"Will you look for him?"

Matthew stepped to the door, opening from behind the bar, and called the name of Frank.

"What's wanted?" growled the boy.

"Is your father in the house?"

"I don't know, nor don't care," was responded in the same ungracious manner.

"Some one bring him into the bar-room, and we'll see if we can't make him care a little."

The suggestion was no sooner made, than two men glided behind the bar, and passed into the room from which the voice of Frank had issued. A moment after they reappeared, each grasping an arm of the boy, and bearing him like a weak child between them. He looked thoroughly frightened at this unlooked-for invasion of his liberty.

"See here, young man." One of the leading spirits of the crowd addressed him, as soon as he was brought in front of the counter. "If you wish to keep out of trouble, answer our questions at once, and to the point. We are in no mood for trifling. Where's your father?"

"Somewhere about the house, I believe," Frank replied, in an humbled tone. He was no little scared at the summary manner with which he had been treated.

"How long since you saw him?"

"Not long ago."

"Ten minutes?"

"No: nearly half an hour."

"Where was he then?"

"He was going up-stairs."

"Very well, we want him. See him, and tell him so."

Frank went into the house, but came back into the bar-room after an absence of nearly five minutes, and said that he could not find his father anywhere.

"Where is he then?" was angrily demanded.

"Indeed, gentlemen, I don't know." Frank's anxious look and frightened manner showed that he spoke truly.

"There's something wrong about this—something wrong—wrong," said one of the men. "Why should he be absent now? Why has he taken no steps to secure the man who committed a murder in his own house, and before his own eyes?"

"I shouldn't wonder if he aided him to escape," said another, making this serious charge with a restlessness and want of evidence that illustrated the reckless and unjust spirit by which a mob is ever governed.

"No doubt of it in the least!" was the quick and positive response. And at once this erroneous conviction seized upon every one. Not a single fact was presented. The simple, bold assertion, that no doubt existed in the

mind of one man as to Slade's having aided
Green to escape, was sufficient for the unre-
flecting mob.

"Where is he? Where is he? Let us find
him. He knows where Green is, and he shall
reveal the secret."

This was enough. The passions of the crowd
were at fever heat again. Two or three men
were chosen to search the house and premises,
while others dispersed to take a wider range.
One of the men who volunteered to go over the
house was a person named Lyon, with whom I
had formed some acquaintance, and several
times conversed with on the state of affairs in
Cedarville. He still remained too good a customer at the bar. I left the bar at the same
time that he did, and went up to my room.
We walked side by side, and parted at my
door, I going in, and he continuing on to make
his searches. I felt, of course, anxious and
much excited, as well in consequence of the
events of the day, as the present aspect of

things. My head was aching violently, and in the hope of getting relief, I laid myself down. I had already lighted a candle, and turned the key in my door to prevent intrusion. Only for a short time did I lie, listening to the hum of voices that came with a hoarse murmur from below, to the sound of feet moving along the passages, and to the continual opening and shutting of doors, when something like suppressed breathing reached my ears. I started up instantly, and listened; but my quickened pulses were now audible to my own sense, and obscured what was external.

"It is only imagination," I said to myself. Still, I sat upright, listening.

Satisfied, at length, that all was mere fancy, I laid myself back on the pillow, and tried to turn my thoughts away from the suggested idea that some one was in the room. Scarcely had I succeeded in this, when my heart gave a new impulse, as a sound like a movement fell upon my ears.

"Mere fancy!" I said to myself, as some one went past the door at the moment. "My mind is over-excited."

Still I raised my head, supporting it with my hand, and listened, directing my attention inside, and not outside of the room. I was about letting my head fall back upon the pillow, when a slight cough, so distinct as not to be mistaken, caused me to spring to the floor, and look under the bed. The mystery was explained. A pair of eyes glittered in the candlelight. The fugitive, Green, was under my bed. For some moments I stood looking at him, so astonished that I had neither utterance nor decision; while he glared at me with a fierce defiance. I saw that he was clutching a revolver.

"Understand!" he said, in a grating whisper, "that I am not to be taken alive."

I let the blanket, which had concealed him from view, fall from my hand, and then tried to collect my thoughts.

"Escape is impossible," said I, again lifting the temporary curtain by which he was hid. "The whole town is armed, and on the search; and should you fall into the hands of the mob, in its present state of exasperation, your life would not be safe an instant. Remain, then, quiet, where you are, until I can see the sheriff, to whom you had better resign yourself, for there's little chance for you except under his protection."

After a brief parley, he consented that things should take this course, and I went out, locking the room door after me, and started in search of the sheriff. On the information I gave, the sheriff acted promptly. With five officers, fully armed for defense, in case an effort were made to get the prisoner out of their hands, he re-paired immediately to the "Sickle and Sheaf." I had given the key of my room into his pos-session.

The appearance of the sheriff, with his *posse*, was sufficient to start the suggestion that Green was somewhere concealed in the house; and a suggestion was only needed to cause the fact to be assumed, and unhesitatingly declared. Intelligence went through the reassembling crowd like an electric current, and ere the sheriff could manacle and lead forth his prisoner, the stairway down which he had to come was packed with bodies, and echoing with oaths and maledictions.

"Gentlemen, clear the way!" cried the sheriff, as he appeared with the white and trembling culprit at the head of the stairs. "The murderer is now in the hands of the law, and will meet the sure consequences of his crime."

A shout of execration rent the air; but not a single individual stirred.

"Give way, there! Give way!" And the sheriff took a step or two forward, but the prisoner held back.

"Oh, the murdering villain! The cursed blackleg! Where's Willy Hammond?" was heard distinctly above the confused mingling of voices.

"Gentlemen! the law must have its course; and no good citizen will oppose the law. It is made for your protection—for mine—and for that of the prisoner."

"Lynch law is good enough for him," shouted a savage voice. "Hand him over to us, sheriff, and we'll save you the trouble of hanging him, and the county the cost of a gallows. We'll do the business right."

Five men, each armed with a revolver, now ranged themselves around the sheriff, and the latter said firmly:

"It is my duty to see this man safely conveyed to prison; and I'm going to do my duty. If there is any more blood shed here, the blame will rest with you." And the body of officers pressed forward, the mob slowly retreating before them.

Green, overwhelmed with terror, held back. I was standing where I could see his face. It was ghastly with mortal fear. Grasping his pinioned arms, the sheriff forced him onward. After contending with the crowd for nearly ten minutes, the officers gained the passage below; but the mob was denser here, and blocking up the door, resolutely maintained their position.

Again and again the sheriff appealed to the good sense and justice of the people.

"The prisoner will have to stand a trial and the law will execute sure vengeance."

"No, it won't!" was sternly responded.

"Who'll be judge in the case?" was asked.

"Why, Judge Lyman!" was contemptuously answered.

"A blackleg himself!" was shouted by two or three voices.

"Blackleg judge, and blackleg lawyers! Oh, yes! The law will execute sure vengeance! Who was in the room gambling with Green and Hammond?"

"Judge Lyman!" "Judge Lyman!" was answered back.

"It won't do, sheriff! There's no law in the country to reach the case but Lynch law; and that the scoundrel must have. Give him to us!"

"Never! On, men, with the prisoner!" cried the sheriff resolutely, and the *posse* made a rush toward the door, bearing back the resisting and now infuriated crowd. Shouts, cries, oaths, and savage imprecations blended in wild discord; in the midst of which my blood was chilled by the sharp crack of a pistol. Another and another shot followed; and then, as a cry of pain thrilled the air, the fierce storm hushed its fury in an instant.

"Who's shot? Is he killed?"

There was a breathless eagerness for the answer.

"It's the gambler!" was replied. "Somebody has shot Green."

A low muttered invective against the victim

was heard here and there; but the announcement was not received with a shout of exulta-
tion, though there was scarcely a heart that
did not feel pleasure at the sacrifice of Harvey
Green's life.

It was true as had been declared. Whether
the shot were aimed deliberately, or guided by
an unseen hand to the heart of the gambler,
was never known; nor did the most careful
examination, instituted afterward by the county, elicit any information that even directed
suspicion toward the individual who became
the agent of his death.

At the coroner's inquest, held over the dead
body of Harvey Green, Simon Slade was present. Where he had concealed himself while
the mob were in search of him, was not known.
He looked haggard; and his eyes were anxious
and restless. Two murders in his house, oc-
curring in a single day, were quite enough
to darken his spirits; and the more so, as
his relations with both the victims were not

of a character to awaken any thing but self-accusation.

As for the mob, in the death of Green its eager thirst for vengeance was satisfied. Nothing more was said against Slade, as a participator in the ruin and death of young Hammond. The popular feeling was one of pity rather than indignation toward the landlord; for it was seen that he was deeply troubled.

One thing I noticed, and it was that the drinking at the bar was not suspended for a moment. A large proportion of those who made up the crowd of Green's angry pursuers were excited by drink as well as indignation, and I am very sure that, but for the maddening effects of liquor, the fatal shot would never have been fired. After the fearful catastrophe, and when every mind was sobered, or ought to have been sobered, the crowd returned to the bar-room, where the drinking was renewed. So rapid were the calls for liquor, that both

Matthew and Frank, the landlord's son, were kept busy mixing the various compounds demanded by the thirsty customers.

From the constant stream of human beings that flowed toward the "Sickle and Sheaf," after the news of Green's discovery and death went forth, it seemed as if every man and boy within a distance of two or three miles had received intelligence of the event. Few, very, of those who came, but went first into the barroom; and nearly all who entered the bar-room called for liquor. In an hour after the death of Green, the fact that his dead body was laid out in the room immediately adjoining, seemed utterly to pass from the consciousness of every one in the bar. The calls for liquor were incessant; and, as the excitement of drink increased, voices grew louder, and oaths more plentiful, while the sounds of laughter ceased not for an instant.

"'They're giving him a regular Irish wake," I heard remarked, with a brutal laugh.

I turned to the speaker, and, to my great surprise, saw that it was Judge Lyman, more under the influence of drink than I remembered
to have seen him. He was about the last man
I expected to find here. If he knew of the
strong indignation expressed toward him a little while before, by some of the very men now
excited with liquor, his own free drinking had
extinguished fear.

"Yes, curse him!" was the answer. "If
they have a particularly hot corner 'away
down below,' I hope he's made its acquaintance
before this."

"Most likely he's smelled brimstone," chuckled the judge.

"Smelled it! If old Clubfoot hasn't treated
him with a brimstone-bath long before this, he
hasn't done his duty. If I thought as much,
I'd vote for sending his majesty a remonstrance
forthwith."

"Ha! ha!" laughed the judge. "You're
warm on the subject."

"Ain't I? The blackleg scoundrel! Hell's too good for him."

"H-u-s-h! Don't let your indignation run into profanity," said Judge Lyman, trying to assume a serious air; but the muscles of his face but feebly obeyed his will's feeble effort.

"Profanity! Poh! I don't call that profanity. It's only speaking out in meeting, as they say,—it's only calling black, black—and white, white. You believe in a hell, don't you, judge?"

"I suppose there is one; though I don't know very certain."

"You'd better be certain!" said the other, meaningly.

"Why so?"

"Oh! because if there is one, and you don't cut your cards a little differently, you'll be apt to find it at the end of your journey."

"What do you mean by that?" asked the judge, retreating somewhat into himself, and trying to look dignified.

"Just what I say," was unhesitatingly answered.

"Do you mean to insinuate any thing?" asked the judge, whose brows were beginning to knit themselves.

"Nobody thinks you a saint," replied the man, roughly.

"I never professed to be."

"And it is said"—the man fixed his gaze almost insultingly upon Judge Lyman's face—"that you'll get about as hot a corner in the lower regions as is to be found there, whenever you make the journey in that direction."

"You are insolent!" exclaimed the judge, his face becoming inflamed.

"Take care what you say, sir!" The man spoke threateningly.

"You'd better take care what *you* say."

"So I will," replied the other. "But——"

"What's to pay here?" inquired a third party, coming up at the moment, and interrupting the speaker.

"The devil will be to pay," said Judge Ly·
man, "if somebody don't look out sharp."

"Do you mean that for me, ha?" The man,
between whom and himself this slight contention had so quickly sprung up, began stripping
back his coat sleeves, like one about to commence boxing.

"I mean it for anybody who presumes to
offer me an insult."

The raised voices of the two men now drew
toward them the attention of every one in the
bar-room.

"The devil! There's Judge Lyman!" I
heard some one exclaim, in a tone of surprise.

"Wasn't he in the room with Green when
Willy Hammond was murdered?" asked another.

"Yes, he was; and what's more, it is said he
had been playing against him all night, he and
Green sharing the plunder."

This last remark came distinctly to the ears

of Lyman, who started to his feet instantly exclaiming fiercely :

"Whoever says that is a cursed liar !"

The words were scarcely out of his mouth, before a blow staggered him against the wall, near which he was standing. Another blow felled him, and then his assailant sprang over his prostrate body, kicking him, and stamping upon his face and breast in the most brutal, shocking manner.

"Kill him ! He's worse than Green !" somebody cried out, in a voice so full of cruelty and murder that it made my blood curdle. "Remember Willy Hammond !"

The terrible scene that followed, in which were heard a confused mingling of blows, cries, yells, and horrible oaths, continued for several minutes, and ceased only when the words— "Don't, don't strike him any more! He's dead !" were repeated several times. Then the wild strife subsided. As the crowd parted from around the body of Judge Lyman, and

gave way, I caught a single glance at his face.
It was covered with blood, and every feature
seemed to have been literally trampled down,
until all was a level surface! Sickened at the
sight, I passed hastily from the room into the
open air, and caught my breath several times,
before respiration again went on freely. As I
stood in front of the tavern, the body of Judge
Lyman was borne out by three or four men,
and carried off in the direction of his dwelling.

"Is he dead?" I inquired of those who had
him in charge.

"No," was the answer. "He's not dead, but
terribly beaten," and they passed on.

Again the loud voices of men in angry strife
arose in the bar-room. I did not return there
to learn the cause, or to witness the fiend-like
conduct of men, all whose worst passions were
stimulated by drink into the wildest fervor.
As I was entering my room, the thought flashed
through my mind that, as Green was found

there, it needed only the bare suggestion that I had aided in his concealment, to direct toward me the insane fury of the drunken mob.

"It is not safe to remain here." I said this to myself, with the emphasis of a strong internal conviction.

Against this, my mind opposed a few feeble arguments; but the more I thought of the matter, the more clearly did I become satisfied, that to attempt to pass the night in that room was to me a risk it was not prudent to assume.

So I went in search of Mrs. Slade, to ask her to have another room prepared for me. But she was not in the house; and I learned, upon inquiry, that since the murder of young Hammond, she had been suffering from repeated hysterical and fainting fits, and was now, with her daughter, at the house of a relative, whither she had been carried early in the afternoon.

It was on my lip to request the chambermaid to give me another room; but this I felt

to be scarcely prudent, for if the popular indignation should happen to turn toward me,
the servant would be the one questioned, most
likely, as to where I had removed my quarters.

"It isn't safe to stay in the house," said I,
speaking to myself. "Two, perhaps three,
murders have been committed already. The
tiger's thirst for blood has been stimulated, and
who can tell how quickly he may spring again,
or in what direction?"

Even while I said this, there came up from
the bar-room louder and madder shouts. Then
blows were heard, mingled with cries and
oaths. A shuddering sense of danger oppressed
me, and I went hastily down-stairs, and out
into the street. As I gained the passage, I
looked into the sitting-room, where the body
of Green was laid out. Just then, the bar-room
door was burst open by a fighting party, who
had been thrown, in their fierce contention,
against it. I paused only for a moment or
two; and even in that brief period of time,

saw blows exchanged over the dead body of the gambler!

"This is no place for me," I said, almost aloud, and hurried from the house, and took my way to the residence of a gentleman who had shown me mary kindnesses during my visits at Cedarville There was needed scarcely a word of representation on my part, to secure the cordial tender of a bed.

What a change! It seemed almost like a passage from Pandemonium to a heavenly region, as I seated myself alone in the quiet chamber a cheerful hospitality had assigned me, and mused on the exciting and terrible incidents of the day. They that sow the wind shall reap the whirlwind. How marked had been the realization of this prophecy, couched in such strong but beautiful imagery!

On the next day I was to leave Cedarville. Early in the morning I repaired to the "Sickle and Sheaf." The storm was over, and all was calm and silent as desolation. Hours before, the tempest had subsided; but the evidences left behind of its ravaging fury were fearful to look upon. Doors, chairs, windows, and tables were broken, and even the strong brass rod that ornamented the bar had been partially wrenched from its fastenings by strong hands, under an impulse of murder, that only lacked a weapon to execute its fiendish purpose. Stains of blood, in drops, marks, and even dried-up pools, were to be seen all over the bar-room and passage floors, and in many places on the porch.

In the sitting-room still lay the body of Green. Here, too, were many signs to indicate a fierce struggle. The looking-glass was smashed to a hundred pieces, and the shivered fragments lay yet untouched upon the floor. A chair, which it was plain had been used as a weapon of assault, had two of its legs broken short off, and was thrown into a corner. And even the bearers on which the dead man lay were pushed from their true position, showing that even in its mortal sleep, the body of Green had felt the jarring strife of elements he had himself helped to awaken into mad activity. From his face, the sheet had been drawn aside; but no hand ventured to replace it; and there it lay, in its ghastly paleness, exposed to the light, and covered with restless flies, attracted by the first faint odors of putridity. With gaze averted, I approached the body, and drew the covering decently over it.

No person was in the bar. I went out into the stable-yard, where I met the hostler with his head bound up. There was a dark blue circle around one of his eyes, and an ugly-looking red scar on his cheek.

"Where is Mr. Slade?" I inquired.

"In bed, and likely to keep it for a week," was answered.

"How comes that?"

"Naturally enough. There was fighting all around last night, and he had to come in for a share. The fool! If he'd just held his tongue, he might have come out of it with a whole skin. But, when the rum is in, the wit is out, with him. It's cost me a black eye and a broken head; for how could I stand by and see him murdered outright?"

"Is he very badly injured?"

"I rather think he is. One eye is clean gone."

"Oh, shocking!"

"It's shocking enough, and no mistake."

"Lost an eye?"

"Too true, sir. The doctor saw him this morning, and says the eye was fairly gouged out, and broken up. In fact, when we carried him up-stairs for dead, last night, his eye was lying upon his cheek. I pushed it back with my own hand!"

"Oh, horrible!" The relation made me sick. "Is he otherwise much injured?"

"The doctor thinks there are some bad hurts inside. Why, they kicked and trampled upon him, as if he had been a wild beast! I never saw such a pack of blood-thirsty devils in my life."

"So much for rum," said I.

"Yes, sir; so much for rum," was the emphatic response. "It was the rum, and nothing else. Why, some of the very men who acted the most like tigers and devils, are as harmless persons as you will find in Cedarville when sober. Yes, sir; it was the rum, and nothing else. Rum gave me this broken head and black eye."

"So you had been drinking also?"

"Oh, yes. There's no use in denying that."

"Liquor does you harm."

"Nobody knows that better than I do."

"Why do you drink, then?"

"Oh, just because it comes in the way. Liquor is under my eyes and nose all the time, and it's as natural as breathing to take a little now and then. And when I don't think of it myself, somebody will think of it

for me, and say—'Come, Sam, let's take something.' So you see, for a body such as I am,
there isn't much help for it."

"But ain't you afraid to go on in this way?
Don't you know where it will all end?"

"Just as well as anybody. It will make an
end of me—or of all that is good in me. Rum
and ruin, you know, sir. They go together
like twin brothers."

"Why don't you get out of the way of
temptation?" said I.

"It's easy enough to ask that question, sir;
but how am I to get out of the way of temptation? Where shall I go, and not find a bar in
my road, and somebody to say—'Come, Sam,
let's take a drink?' It can't be done, sir, no-
how. I'm a hostler, and don't know how to be
any thing else."

"Can't you work on a farm?"

"Yes; I can do something in that way.
But, when there are taverns and bar-rooms,
as many as three or four in every mile all over

the country, how are you to keep clear of them?
Figure me out that."

"I think you'd better vote on the Maine
Law side at next election," said I.

"Faith, and I did it last time!" replied the
man, with a brightening face—"and if I'm
spared, I'll go the same ticket next year.'

"What do you think of the Law?" I asked.

"Think of it! Bless your heart! if I was a
praying man, which I'm sorry to say I ain't—
my mother was a pious woman, sir"—his voice
fell and slightly trembled—"if I was a praying
man, sir, I'd pray, night and morning, and
twenty times every day of my life, for God to
put it into the hearts of the people to give us
that Law. I'd have some hope then. But I
haven't much as it is. There's no use in trying to let liquor alone."

"Do many drinking men think as you do?"

"I can count up a dozen or two myself. It
isn't the drinking men who are so much opposed to the Maine Law as your politicians.

They throw dust in the people's eyes about it, and make a great many, who know nothing at all of the evils of drinking in themselves, believe some bugbear story about trampling on the rights of I don't know who, nor they either. As for rum-sellers' rights, I never could see any right they had to get rich by ruining poor devils such as I am. I think, though, that we have some right to be protected against them."

The ringing of a bell here announced the arrival of some traveler, and the hostler left me.

I learned, during the morning, that Matthew, the bar-keeper, and also the son of Mr. Slade, were both considerably hurt during the affrays in the bar-room, and were confined, temporarily, to their beds. Mrs. Slade still continued in a distressing and dangerous state. Judge Lyman, though shockingly injured, was not thought to be in a critical condition.

A busy day the sheriff had of it, making arrests of various parties engaged in the last

night's affairs. Even Slade, unable as he was
to lift his head from his pillow, was required
to give heavy bail for his appearance at court.
Happily, I escaped the inconvenience of being
held to appear as a witness, and early in the
afternoon had the satisfaction of finding myself
rapidly borne away in the stage-coach. It was
two years before I entered the pleasant village
of Cedarville again.

19

NIGHT THE EIGHTH.

REAPING THE WHIRLWIND.

I WAS in Washington City during the succeeding month. It was the short, or closing session of a regular Congressional term. The implication of Judge Lyman in the affair of Green and young Hammond had brought him into such bad odor in Cedarville, and the whole district from which he had been chosen, that his party deemed it wise to set him aside, and take up a candidate less likely to meet with so strong, and, it might be, successful an opposition. By so doing, they were able to secure the election, once more, against the growing temperance party, which succeeded, however, in getting a Maine Law man into the State Legislature. It was, therefore, Judge Lyman's last winter at the Federal Capital.

While seated in the reading-room at Fuller's Hotel, about noon, on the day after my arrival in Washington, I noticed an individual, whose face looked familiar, come in and glance about, as if in search of some one. While yet questioning in my mind who he could be, I heard a man remark to a person with whom he had been conversing:

"There's that vagabond member away from his place in the House, again."

"Who?" inquired the other.

"Why, Judge Lyman," was answered.

"Oh!" said the other, indifferently; "it isn't of much consequence. Precious little wisdom does he add to that intelligent body."

"His vote is worth something, at least, when important questions are at stake."

"What does he charge for it?" was coolly inquired.

There was a shrug of the shoulders, and an arching of the eyebrows, but no answer.

"I'm in earnest, though, in the question,' said the last speaker.

"Not in saying that Lyman will sell his vote to the highest bidders?"

"That will depend altogether upon whom the bidders may be. They must be men who have something to lose as well as gain—men not at all likely to bruit the matter, and in serving whose personal interests no abandonment of party is required. Judge Lyman is always on good terms with the lobby members, and may be found in company with some of them daily. Doubtless, his absence from the House, now, is for the purpose of a special meeting with gentlemen who are ready to pay well for votes in favor of some bill making appropriations of public money for private or corporate benefit."

"You certainly can not mean all you say to be taken in its broadest sense," was replied to this.

"Yes; in its very broadest. Into just this

deep of moral and political degradation has this man fallen, disgracing his constituents, and dishonoring his country."

"His presence at Washington doesn't speak very highly in favor of the community he represents."

"No; still, as things are now, we cannot judge of the moral worth of a community by the men sent from it to Congress. Representatives show merely the strength of parties. The candidate chosen in party primary meetings is not selected because he is the best man they have, and the one fittest to legislate wisely in national affairs; but he who happens to have the strongest personal friends among those who nominate, or who is most likely to poll the highest vote. This is why we find, in Congress, such a large preponderance of tenth-rate men."

"A man such as you represent Judge Lyman to be would sell his country, like another Arnold."

"Yes; if the bid were high enough."

"Does he gamble?"

"Gambling, I might say, is a part of his profession. Very few nights pass, I am told, without finding him at the gaming-table."

I heard no more. At all this, I was not in the least surprised; for my knowledge of the man's antecedents had prepared me for allegations quite as bad as these.

During the week I spent at the Federal Capital, I had several opportunities of seeing Judge Lyman, in the House and out of it,—in the House only when the yeas and nays were called on some important measure, or a vote taken on a bill granting special privileges. In the latter case, his vote, as I noticed, was generally cast on the affirmative side. Several times I saw him staggering on the Avenue, and once brought into the House for the purpose of voting, in so drunken a state, that he had to be supported to his seat. And even worse than this—when his name was called, he was asleep, and had to be shaken several times before he was sufficiently aroused to give his vote!

Happily, for the good of his country, it was his last winter in Washington. At the next session, a better man took his place.

Two years from the period of my last visit to Cedarville, I found myself approaching that quiet village again. As the church-spire came in view, and house after house became visible, here and there, standing out in pleasant relief against the green background of woods and fields, all the exciting events which rendered my last visit so memorable, came up fresh in my mind. I was yet thinking of Willy Hammond's dreadful death, and of his broken-hearted mother, whose life went out with his, when the stage rolled by their old homestead. Oh, what a change was here! Neglect, decay, and dilapidation were visible, let the eye fall where it would. The fences were down, here

and there; the hedges, once so green and
nicely trimmed, had grown rankly in some
places, but were stunted and dying in others;
all the beautiful walks were weedy and grass-
grown, and the box-borders dead; the garden,
rainbow-hued in its wealth of choice and beautiful flowers when I first saw it, was lying
waste,—a rooting-ground for hogs. A glance
at the house showed a broken chimney, the
bricks unremoved from the spot where they
struck the ground; a moss-grown roof, with a
large limb from a lightning-rent tree lying
almost balanced over the eaves, and threatening to fall at the touch of the first wind-storm
that swept over. Half of the vines that clam-
bered about the portico were dead, and the
rest, untrained, twined themselves in wild dis-
order, or fell groveling to the earth. One of
the pillars of the portico was broken, as were,
also, two of the steps that went up to it. The
windows of the house were closed, but the
door stood open, and, as the stage went past,

my eyes rested, for a moment, upon an old man seated in the hall. He was not near enough to the door for me to get a view of his face; but the white flowing hair left me in no doubt as to his identity. It was Judge Hammond.

The "Sickle and Sheaf" was yet the stage-house of Cedarville, and there, a few minutes afterward, I found myself. The hand of change had been here also. The first object that attracted my attention was the sign-post, which, at my earlier arrival, some eight or nine years before, stood up in its new white garment of paint, as straight as a plummet-line, bearing proudly aloft the golden sheaf and gleaming sickle. Now, the post, dingy and shattered, and worn from the frequent contact of wheels, and gnawing of restless horses, leaned from its trim perpendicular at an angle of many degrees, as if ashamed of the faded, weather-worn, lying symbol it bore aloft in the sunshine. Around the post was a filthy mud-pool, in which a hog

lay grunting out its sense of enjoyment. Two
or three old empty whisky barrels lumbered
up the dirty porch, on which a coarse, bloated,
vulgar-looking man sat leaning against the
wall—his chair tipped back on its hind legs—
squinting at me from one eye, as I left the stage
and came forward toward the house.

"Ah! is this you?" said he, as I came near
to him, speaking thickly, and getting up with
a heavy motion. I now recognized the altered
person of Simon Slade. On looking at him
closer, I saw that the eye which I had thought
only shut was in fact destroyed. How vividly,
now, uprose in imagination the scenes I had
witnessed during my last night in his bar-room;
the night when a brutal mob, whom he had ine-
briated with liquor, came near murdering him.

"Glad to see you once more, my boy! Glad
to see you! I—I—I'm not just—you see. How
are you? How are you?"

And he shook my hand with a drunken
show of cordiality.

I felt shocked and disgusted. Wretched man! down the crumbling sides of the pit he had digged for other feet, he was himself sliding, while not enough strength remained even to struggle with his fate.

I tried for a few minutes to talk with him; but his mind was altogether beclouded, and his questions and answers incoherent; so I left him, and entered the bar-room.

"Can I get accommodations here for a couple of days?" I inquired of a stupid, sleepy-looking man, who was sitting in a chair behind the bar.

"I reckon so," he answered, but did not rise.

I turned, and walked a few paces toward the door, and then walked back again.

"I'd like to get a room," said I.

The man got up slowly, and going to a desk, fumbled about in it for a while. At length he brought out an old, dilapidated blank-book, and throwing it open on the counter, asked me, with an indifferent manner, to write down my name.

"I'll take a pen, if you please."

"Oh, yes!" And he hunted about again in the desk, from which, after a while, he brought forth the blackened stump of a quill, and pushed it toward me across the counter.

"Ink," said I—fixing my eyes upon him with a look of displeasure.

"I don't believe there is any," he muttered. "Frank," and he called the landlord's son, going to the door behind the bar as he did so.

"What d'ye want?" a rough, ill-natured voice answered.

"Where's the ink?"

"Don't know any thing about it."

"You had it last. What did you do with it?"

"Nothing!" was growled back.

"Well, I wish you'd find it."

"Find it yourself, and——" I cannot repeat the profane language he used.

"Never mind," said I. "A pencil will do just as well." And I drew one from my pocket. The attempt to write with this, on the begrimed and greasy page of the register, was only partially successful. It would have puzzled almost any one to make out the name. From the date of the last entry, it appeared that mine was the first arrival, for over a week, of any person desiring a room.

As I finished writing my name, Frank came stalking in, with a cigar in his mouth, and a cloud of smoke around his head. He had grown into a stout man—though his face presented little that was manly, in the true sense of the word. It was disgustingly sensual. On seeing me, a slight flush tinged his cheeks.

"How do you do?" he said, offering me his hand. "Peter,"—he turned to the lazy-looking bar-keeper—"tell Jane to have No. 11 put in order for a gentleman immediately, and tell her to be sure and change the bed-linen."

"Things look rather dull here," I remarked,

as the bar-keeper went out to do as he had been directed.

"Rather; it's a dull place, anyhow."

"How is your mother?" I inquired.

A slight, troubled look came into his face, as he answered:

"No better."

"She's sick, then?"

"Yes; she's been sick a good while; and I'm afraid will never be much better." His manner was not altogether cold and indifferent, but there was a want of feeling in his voice.

"Is she at home?"

"No, sir."

As he showed no inclination to say more on the subject, I asked no further questions, and he soon found occasion to leave me.

The bar-room had undergone no material change, so far as its furniture and arrangements were concerned; but a very great change was apparent in the condition of these. The brass rod around the bar, which, at my last visit, was brightly polished, was now a green-ish-black, and there came from it an unpleasant odor of verdigris. The walls were fairly coated with dust, smoke, and fly-specks, and the win-dows let in the light but feebly through the dirt-obscured glass. The floor was filthy. Be-hind the bar, on the shelves designed for a dis-play of liquors, was a confused mingling of empty or half-filled decanters, cigar-boxes, lemons and lemon-peel, old newspapers, glasses, a broken pitcher, a hat, a soiled vest, and a pair of blacking-brushes, with other incongru-ous things, not now remembered. The air of the room was loaded with offensive vapors.

Disgusted with every thing about the bar, I went into the sitting-room. Here, there was some order in the arrangement of the dingy furniture; but you might have written your name in dust on the looking-glass and table. The smell of the torpid atmosphere was even worse than that of the bar-room. So I did not linger here, but passed through the hall, and out upon the porch, to get a draught of pure air.

Slade still sat leaning against the wall.

"Fine day this," said he, speaking in a mumbling kind of voice.

"Very fine," I answered.

"Yes, very fine."

"Not doing so well as you were a few years ago," said I.

"No—you see—these—these 'ere blamed temperance people are ruining every thing."

"Ah! Is that so?"

"Yes. Cedarville isn't what it was when you first came to the 'Sickle and Sheaf.' I— I—you see. Curse the temperance people! They've ruined every thing, you see. Every thing! Ruined——"

And he muttered, and mouthed his words in such a way, that I could understand but little he said; and, in that little, there was scarcely any coherency. So I left him, with a feeling of pity in my heart for the wreck he had be-

come, and went into the town to call upon one
or two gentlemen with whom I had business.

In the course of the afternoon, I learned that
Mrs. Slade was in an insane asylum, about five
miles from Cedarville. The terrible events of
the day on which young Hammond was murdered completed the work of mental ruin, begun at the time her husband abandoned the
quiet, honorable calling of a miller, and became
a tavern-keeper. Reason could hold its position no longer. When word came to her that
Willy and his mother were both dead, she uttered a wild shriek, and fell down in a fainting
fit. From that period the balance of her mind
was destroyed. Long before this, her friends
saw that reason wavered. Frank had been her
idol. A pure, bright, affectionate boy he was,
when she removed with him from their pleasant cottage-home, where all the surrounding
influences were good, into a tavern, where an
angel could scarcely remain without corruption. From the moment this change was
20

decided on by her husband, a shadow fell upon her heart. She saw, before her husband, her children, and herself, a yawning pit, and felt that, in a very few years, all of them must plunge down into its fearful darkness.

Alas! how quickly began the realization of her worst fears in the corruption of her worshiped boy! And how vain proved all effort and remonstrance, looking to his safety, whether made with himself or his father! From the day the tavern was opened, and Frank drew into his lungs full draughts of the changed atmosphere by which he was now surrounded, the work of moral deterioration commenced. The very smell of the liquor exhilarated him unnaturally; while the subjects of conversation, so new to him, that found discussion in the bar-room, soon came to occupy a prominent place in his imagination, to the exclusion of those humane, child-like, tender, and heavenly thoughts and impressions it had been the mother's care to impart and awaken.

Ah! with what an eager zest does the heart drink in of evil. And how almost hopeless is the case of a boy, surrounded, as Frank was, by the corrupting, debasing associations of a bar-room! Had his father meditated his ruin, he could not have more surely laid his plans for the fearful consummation; and he reaped as he had sown. With a selfish desire to get gain, he embarked in the trade of corruption, ruin, and death, weakly believing that he and his could pass through the fire harmless. How sadly a few years demonstrated his error, we have seen.

Flora, I learned, was with her mother, devoting her life to her. The dreadful death of Willy Hammond, for whom she had conceived a strong attachment, came near depriving her of reason also. Since the day on which that awful tragedy occurred, she had never even looked upon her old home. She went away with her unconscious mother, and ever since had remained with her—devoting her life to

her comfort. Long before this, all her own
and mother's influence over her brother had
come to an end. It mattered not how she
sought to stay his feet, so swiftly moving along
the downward way, whether by gentle en-
treaty, earnest remonstrance, or tears; in either
case, wounds for her own heart were the sure
consequences, while his steps never lingered a
moment. A swift destiny seemed hurrying
him on to ruin. The change in her father—
once so tender, so cheerful in his tone, so proud
of and loving toward his daughter—was another source of deep grief to her pure young
spirit. Over him, as well as over her brother,
all her power was lost; and he even avoided
her, as though her presence were an offense to
him. And so, when she went out from her unhappy home, she took with her no desire to
return. Even when imagination bore her back
to the "Sickle and Sheaf," she felt an intense,
heart-sickening repulsion toward the place
where she had first felt the poisoned arrows of

life; and in the depths of her spirit she prayed that her eyes might never look upon it again. In her almost cloister-like seclusion, she sought to gather the mantle of oblivion about her heart.

Had not her mother's condition made Flora's duty a plain one, the true, unselfish instincts of her heart would have doubtless led her back to the polluted home she had left, there, in a kind of living death, to minister as best she could to the comfort of a debased father and brother. But she was spared that trial—that fruitless sacrifice.

Evening found me once more in the bar-room of the "Sickle and Sheaf." The sleepy, indifferent bar-keeper, was now more in his element —looked brighter, and had quicker motions. Slade, who had partially recovered from the stupefying effects of the heavy draughts of ale with which he washed down his dinner, was also in a better condition, though not inclined to talk. He was sitting at a table, alone, with his eyes wandering about the room. Whether his thoughts were agreeable or disagreeable, it was not easy to determine. Frank was there, the centre of a noisy group of coarse fellows, whose vulgar sayings and profane expletives continually rung through the room. The noisiest, coarsest, and most profane was Frank Slade; yet did not the incessant volume of bad language that flowed from his tongue appear in the least to disturb his father.

Outraged, at length, by this disgusting exhibition, that had not even the excuse of an exciting cause, I was leaving the bar-room, when I heard some one remark to a young man who had just come in:

"What! you here again, Ned? Ain't you afraid your old man will be after you, as usual?"

"No," answered the person addressed, chucking inwardly, "he's gone to a prayer-meeting."

"You'll at least have the benefit of his prayers," was lightly remarked.

I turned to observe the young man more closely. His face I remembered, though I could not identify him at first. But, when I heard him addressed soon after as Ned Hargrove, I had a vivid recollection of a little incident that occurred some years before, and which then made a strong impression. The reader has hardly forgotten the visit of Mr. Hargrove to the bar-room of the "Sickle and Sheaf," and the conversation among some of its inmates, which his withdrawal, in company with his son, then occasioned. The father's watchfulness over his boy, and his efforts to save him from the allurements and temptations of a bar-room, had proved, as now appeared, unavailing. The son was several years older; but it was sadly evident, from the expression of his face, that he had been growing older in evil faster than in years.

The few words that I have mentioned as passing between this young man and another inmate of the bar-room, caused me to turn back from the door, through which I was about passing, and take a chair near to where Hargrove had seated himself. As I did so, the eyes of Simon Slade rested on the last-named individual.

"Ned Hargrove!" he said, speaking roughly —"if you want a drink, you'd better get it, and make yourself scarce."

"Don't trouble yourself," retorted the young man, "you'll get your money for the drink in good time."

This irritated the landlord, who swore at Hargrove violently, and said something about not wanting boys about his place who couldn't stir from home without having "daddy or mammy running after them."

"Never fear!" cried out the person who had first addressed Hargrove—"his old man's gone to a prayer-meeting. We shan't have the light of his pious countenance here to-night."

I fixed my eyes upon the young man to see what effect this coarse and irreverent allusion to his father would have. A slight tinge of shame was in his face; but I saw that he had not sufficient moral courage to resent the shameful desecration of a parent's name. How should he, when he was himself the first to desecrate that name?

"If he were forty fathoms deep in the infernal regions," answered Slade, "he'd find out that Ned was here, and get half an hour's leave of absence to come after him. The fact is, I'm tired of seeing his solemn, sanctimonious face here every night. If the boy hasn't spirit enough to tell him to mind his own business, as I have done more than fifty times, why, let the boy stay away himself."

"Why don't you send him off with a flea in his ear, Ned?" said one of the company, a young man scarcely his own age. "My old man tried that game with me, but he soon found that I could hold the winning cards."

"Just what I'm going to do the very next time he comes after me."

"Oh, yes! So you've said twenty times," remarked Frank Slade, in a sneering, insolent manner.

Edward Hargrove had not the spirit to resent this; he only answered:

"Just let him show himself here to-night, and you will see."

"No, we won't see," sneered Frank.

"Wouldn't it be fun!" was exclaimed. "I hope to be on hand, should it ever come off."

"He's as 'fraid as death of the old chap," laughed a sottish-looking man, whose age ought to have inspired him with some respect for the relation between father and son, and doubtless would, had not a long course of drinking and familiarity with debasing associates blunted his moral sense.

"Now for it!" I heard uttered, in a quick, delighted voice. "Now for fun! Spunk up to him, Ned! Never say die!"

I turned toward the door, and there stood the father of Edward Hargrove. How well I remembered the broad, fine forehead, the steady, yet mild eyes, the firm lips, the elevated, superior bearing of the man I had once before seen in that place, and on a like errand. His form was slightly bent now; his hair was whiter; his eyes farther back in his head; his face thinner and marked with deeper lines; and there was in the whole expression of his face a touching sadness. Yet, superior to the marks of time and suffering, an unflinching resolution was visible in his countenance, that gave to it a dignity, and extorted involuntary respect. He stood still, after advancing a few paces, and then, his searching eyes having discovered his son, he said mildly, yet firmly, and with such a strength of parental love in his voice that resistance was scarcely possible:

"Edward! Edward! Come, my son."

"Don't go." The words were spoken in an under-tone, and he who uttered them turned his face away from Mr. Hargrove, so that the old man could not see the motion of his lips.

A little while before, he had spoken bravely against the father of Edward; now, he could not stand up in his presence.

I looked at Edward. He did not move from where he was sitting, and yet I saw that to resist his father cost him no light struggle.

"Edward." There was nothing imperative —nothing stern—nothing commanding in the father's voice; but its great, its almost irresistible power, lay in its expression of the father's belief that his son would instantly leave the place. And it was this power that prevailed. Edward arose, and, with eyes cast upon the floor, was moving away from his companions, when Frank Slade exclaimed:

"Poor, weak fool!"

It was a lightning flash of indignation, rather than a mere glance from the human eye, that Mr. Hargrove threw instantly upon Frank; while his fine form sprung up erect. He did not speak, but merely transfixed him with a look. Frank curled his lip impotently, as he tried to return the old man's withering glances.

"Now look here!" said Simon Slade, in some wrath, "there's been just about enough of this. I'm getting tired of it. Why don't you keep Ned at home? Nobody wants him here."

"Refuse to sell him liquor," returned Mr. Hargrove.

"It's my trade to sell liquor," answered Slade, boldly.

"I wish you had a more honorable calling," said Hargrove, almost mournfully.

"If you insult my father, I'll strike you down!" exclaimed Frank Slade, starting up and assuming a threatening aspect.

"I respect filial devotion, meet it where I will," calmly replied Mr. Hargrove,—"I only wish it had a better foundation in this case. I only wish the father had merited——"

I will not stain my page with the fearful oath that Frank Slade yelled, rather than uttered, as, with clenched fist, he sprung toward Mr. Hargrove. But ere he had reached the unruffled old man—who stood looking at him as one would look into the eyes of a wild beast, confident that he could not stand the gaze—a firm hand grasped his arm, and a rough voice said :

"Avast, there, young man! Touch a hair of that white head, and I'll wring your neck off."

"Lyon!" As Frank uttered the man's name, he raised his fist to strike him. A moment the clenched hand remained poised in the air; then it fell slowly to his side, and he contented himself with an oath and a vile epithet.

"You can swear to your heart's content. It will do nobody any harm but yourself," coolly replied Mr. Lyon, whom I now recognized as the person with whom I had held several conversations during previous visits.

"Thank you, Mr. Lyon," said Mr. Hargrove,

"for this manly interference. It is no more than I should have expected from you."

"I never suffer a young man to strike an old man," said Lyon, firmly. "Apart from that, Mr. Hargrove, there are other reasons why your person must be free from violence where I am."

"This is a bad place for you, Lyon," said Mr. Hargrove; "and I've said so to you a good many times." He spoke in rather an undertone. "Why *will* you come here?"

"It's a bad place, I know," replied Lyon, speaking out boldly, "and we all know it. But habit, Mr. Hargrove—habit. That's the cursed thing! If the bar-rooms were all shut up, there would be another story to tell. Get us the Maine law, and there will be some chance for us."

"Why don't you vote the temperance ticket?" asked Mr. Hargrove.

"Why did I? you'd better ask," said Lyon.

"I thought you voted against us."

"Not I. Ain't quite so blind to my own interests as that. And, if the truth were known, I should not at all wonder if every man in this room, except Slade and his son, voted on your side of the house."

"It's a little strange, then," said Mr. Hargrove, "that with the drinking men on our side, we failed to secure the election."

"You must blame that on your moderate men, who see no danger and go blind with their party," answered Lyon. "We have looked the evil in the face, and know its direful quality."

"Come! I would like to talk with you, Mr. Lyon."

Mr. Hargrove, his son, and Mr. Lyon went out together. As they left the room, Frank Slade said:

"What a cursed liar and hypocrite he is!"

"Who?" was asked.

"Why, Lyon," answered Frank, boldly.

"You'd better say that to his face."

"It wouldn't be good for him," remarked one of the company.

At this Frank started to his feet, stalked about the room, and put on all the disgusting airs of a drunken braggart. Even his father saw the ridiculous figure he cut, and growled out:

"There, Frank, that'll do. Don't make a miserable fool of yourself!"

At which Frank retorted, with so much of insolence that his father flew into a towering passion, and ordered him to leave the bar-room.

"You can go out yourself if you don't like the company. I'm very well satisfied," answered Frank.

"Leave this room, you impudent young scoundrel!"

"Can't go, my amiable friend," said Frank, with a cool self-possession that maddened his father, who got up hastily, and moved across the bar-room to the place where he was standing.

"Go out, I tell you!" Slade spoke resolutely.

21

"Would be happy to oblige you," Frank said, in a taunting voice; "but, 'pon my word, it isn't at all convenient."

Half intoxicated as he was, and already nearly blind with passion, Slade lifted his hand to strike his son. And the blow would have fallen had not some one caught his arm, and held him back from the meditated violence. Even the debased visitors of this bar-room could not stand by and see nature outraged in a bloody strife between father and son; for it was plain from the face and quickly assumed attitude of Frank, that if his father had laid his hand upon him, he would have struck him in return.

I could not remain to hear the awful imprecations that father and son, in their impotent rage, called down from heaven upon each other's heads. It was the most shocking exhibition of depraved human nature that I had ever seen. And so I left the bar-room, glad to escape from its stifling atmosphere and revolting scenes.

NIGHT THE NINTH.

A FEARFUL CONSUMMATION.

NEITHER Slade nor his son was present at the breakfast-table on the next morning. As for myself, I did not eat with much appetite. Whether this defect arose from the state of my mind, or the state of the food set before me, I did not stop to inquire; but left the stifling, offensive atmosphere of the dining-room in a very few moments after entering that usually attractive place for a hungry man.

A few early drinkers were already in the bar-room—men with shattered nerves and cadaverous faces, who could not begin the day's work without the stimulus of brandy or whisky. They came in, with gliding foot-steps, asked for what they wanted in low voices, drank in silence, and departed. It was a melancholy sight to look upon.

About nine o'clock the landlord made his appearance. He, too, came gliding into the bar-room, and his first act was to seize upon a brandy decanter, pour out nearly half a pint of the fiery liquid, and drink it off. How badly his hand shook—so badly that he spilled the brandy both in pouring it out and in lifting the glass to his lips! What a shattered wreck he was! He looked really worse now than he did on the day before, when drink gave an artificial vitality to his system, a tension to his muscles, and light to his countenance. The miller of ten years ago, and the tavern-keeper of to-day! Who could have identified them as one?

Slade was turning from the bar, when a man came in. I noticed an instant change in the landlord's countenance. He looked startled; almost frightened. The man drew a small package from his pocket, and after selecting a paper therefrom, presented it to Slade, who received it with a nervous reluctance, opened, and let his eye fall upon the writing within. I was observing him closely at the time, and saw his countenance flush deeply. In a moment or two it became pale again—paler even than before.

"Very well—all right. I'll attend to it," said the landlord, trying to recover himself, yet swallowing with every sentence.

The man, who was no other than a sheriff's deputy, and who gave him a sober, professional look, then went out with a firm step, and an air of importance. As he passed through the outer door, Slade retired from the bar-room.

"Trouble coming," I heard the bar-keeper remark, speaking partly to himself and partly with the view, as was evident from his manner, of leading me to question him. But this I did not feel that it was right to do.

"Got the sheriff on him at last," added the bar-keeper.

"What's the matter, Bill?" inquired a man who now came in with a bustling, important air, and leaned familiarly over the bar. "Who was Jenkins after?"

"The old man," replied the bar-keeper, in a voice that showed pleasure rather than regret.

"No!"

"It's a fact." Bill, the bar-keeper, actually smiled.

"What's to pay?" said the man.

"Don't know, and don't care much."

"Did he serve a summons or an execution?"

"Can't tell."

"Judge Lyman's suit went against him."

"Did it?"

"Yes; and I heard Judge Lyman swear, that if he got him on the hip, he'd sell him out, bag and basket. And he's the man to keep his word."

"I never could just make out," said the bar-keeper, "how he ever came to owe Judge Lyman so much. I've never known of any business transactions between them."

"It's been dog eat dog, I rather guess," said the man.

"What do you mean by that?" inquired the bar-keeper.

"You've heard of dogs hunting in pairs?"

"Oh, yes."

"Well, since Harvey Green got his deserts, the business of fleecing our silly young fellows, who happened to have more money than wit or discretion, has been in the hands of Judge Lyman and Slade. They hunted together, Slade holding the game, while the Judge acted as blood-sucker. But that business was interrupted about a year ago; and game got so scarce that, as I suggested, dog began to eat dog. And here comes the end of the matter, if I'm not mistaken. So mix us a stiff toddy. I want one more good drink at the 'Sickle and Sheaf,' before the colors are struck."

And the man chuckled at his witty effort.

During the day, I learned that affairs stood pretty much as this man had conjectured. Lyman's suits had been on sundry notes payable on demand; but nobody knew of any property transactions between him and Slade. On the part of Slade, no defense had been made—the suit going by default. The visit of the sheriff's officer was for the purpose of serving an execution.

As I walked through Cedarville on that day, the whole aspect of the place seemed changed. I questioned with myself, often, whether this were really so, or only the effect of imagination. The change was from cheerfulness and thrift, to gloom and neglect. There was, to me, a brooding silence in the air; a pause in the life-movement; a folding of the hands, so to speak, because hope had failed from the heart. The residence of Mr. Harrison, who, some two years before, had suddenly awakened to a lively sense of the evil of rum-selling, because his own sons were discovered to be in danger, had been one of the most tasteful in Cedarville. I had often stopped to admire the beautiful shrubbery and flowers with which it was surrounded; the walks so clear—the borders so fresh and even—the arbors so cool and inviting. There was not a spot upon which the eye could rest, that did not show the hand of taste. When I now came opposite to this house, I was no longer in doubt as to the actuality of a change. There were no marked evidences of neglect; but the high cultivation and nice regard for the small details were lacking. The walks were cleanly swept; but the box-borders were not so carefully trimmed. The vines and bushes that in former times were cut and tied so evenly, could hardly have felt the keen touch of the pruning-knife for months.

As I paused to note the change, a lady, somewhat beyond the middle age, came from the house. I was struck by the deep gloom that overshadowed her countenance. Ah! said I to myself, as I passed on, how many dear hopes, that once lived in that heart, must have been scattered to the winds. As I conjectured, this was Mrs. Harrison, and I was not unprepared to hear, as I did a few hours afterward, that her two sons had fallen into drinking habits; and, not only this, had been enticed to the gaming-table. Unhappy mother! What a life-time of wretchedness was compressed for thee into a few short years!

I walked on, noting, here and there, changes even more marked than appeared about the residence of Mr. Harrison. Judge Lyman's beautiful place showed utter neglect; and so did one or two others that, on my first visit to Cedarville, charmed me with their order, neatness, and cultivation. In every instance, I learned, on inquiring, that the owners of these, or some members of their families, were, or had been, visitors at the "Sickle and Sheaf;" and that the ruin, in progress or completed, began after the establishment of that point of attraction in the village.

Something of a morbid curiosity, excited by

what I saw, led me on to take a closer view of the residence of Judge Hammond than I had obtained on the day before. The first thing that I noticed, on approaching the old, decay-ing mansion, were handbills, posted on the gate, the front-door, and on one of the windows. A nearer inspection revealed their import. The property had been seized, and was now offered at sheriff's sale !

Ten years before, Judge Hammond was known as the richest man in Cedarville: and now, the homestead he had once so loved to beautify—where all that was dearest to him in life once gathered—worn, disfigured, and in ruins, was about being wrested from him. I paused at the gate, and leaning over it, looked in with saddened feelings upon the dreary waste within. No sign of life was visible. The door was shut—the windows closed—not the faintest wreath of smoke was seen above the blackened chimney-tops. How vividly did imagination restore the life, and beauty, and

happiness, that made their home there only a
few years before,—the mother and her noble
boy, one looking with trembling hope, the
other with joyous confidence, into the future,—
the father, proud of his household treasures,
but not their wise and jealous guardian.

Ah! that his hands should have unbarred
the door, and thrown it wide, for the wolf to
enter that precious fold! I saw them all in
their sunny life before me; yet, even as I
looked upon them, their sky began to darken.
I heard the distant mutterings of the storm,
and soon the desolating tempest swept down
fearfully upon them. I shuddered as it passed
away, to look upon the wrecks left scattered
around. What a change!

"And all this," said I, "that one man, tired
of being useful, and eager to get gain, might
gather in accursed gold!"

Pushing open the gate, I entered the yard,
and walked around the dwelling, my foot-
steps echoing in the hushed solitude of the

deserted place. Hark! was that a human voice?

I paused to listen.

The sound came, once more, distinctly to my ears. I looked around, above, everywhere, but perceived no living sign. For nearly a minute I stood still, listening. Yes: there it was again—a low, moaning voice, as of one in pain or grief. I stepped onward a few paces; and now saw one of the doors standing ajar. As I pushed this door wide open, the moan was repeated. Following the direction from which the sound came, I entered one of the large drawing-rooms. The atmosphere was stifling, and all as dark as if it were midnight. Groping my way to a window, I drew back the bolt and threw open a shutter. Broadly the light fell across the dusty, uncarpeted floor, and on the dingy furniture of the room. As it did so, the moaning voice which had drawn me thither swelled on the air again; and now I saw, lying upon an old sofa, the form of a man. It needed no second glance to tell me that this was Judge Hammond. I put my hand upon him, and uttered his name: but he answered not. I spoke more firmly, and slightly shook him; but only a piteous moan was returned.

"Judge Hammond!" I now called aloud, and somewhat imperatively.

But it availed nothing. The poor old man aroused not from the stupor in which mind and body were enshrouded.

"He is dying!" thought I; and instantly left the house in search of some friends to take charge of him in his last, sad extremity. The first person to whom I made known the fact shrugged his shoulders, and said it was no affair of his, and that I must find somebody whose business it was to attend to him. My next application was met in the same spirit; and no better success attended my reference of the matter to a third party. No one to whom I spoke seemed to have any sympathy for the broken-down old man. Shocked by this indifference, I went to one of the county officers, who, on learning the condition of Judge Hammond, took immediate steps to have him removed to the Alms-house, some miles distant.

"But why to the Alms-house?" I inquired, on learning his purpose. "He has property."

"Every thing has been seized for debt," was the reply.

"Will there be nothing left after his creditors are satisfied?"

"Very few, if any, will be satisfied," he answered. "There will not be enough to pay half the judgments against him."

"And is there no friend to take him in,—no one, of all who moved by his side in the days of prosperity, to give a few hours' shelter, and soothe the last moments of his unhappy life?"

"Why did you make application here?" was the officer's significant question.

I was silent.

"Your earnest appeals for the poor old man met with no words of sympathy?"

"None."

"He has, indeed, fallen low. In the days of his prosperity, he had many friends, so called. Adversity has shaken them all like dead leaves from sapless branches."

"But why? This is not always so."

"Judge Hammond was a selfish, worldly man. People never liked him much. His favoring, so strongly, the tavern of Slade, and his distillery operations, turned from him some of his best friends. The corruption and terrible fate of his son—and the insanity and death of his wife—all were charged upon him in people's minds; and every one seemed to turn from him instinctively after the fearful tragedy was completed. He never held up his head afterward. Neighbors shunned him as they would a criminal. And here has come the end at last. He will be taken to the Poor-house, to die there—a pauper!"

"And all," said I, partly speaking to my-self, "because a man, too lazy to work at an honest calling, must needs go to rum-selling."

"The truth, the whole truth, and nothing but the truth," remarked the officer with emphasis, as he turned from me to see that his directions touching the removal of Mr. Hammond to the Poor-house were promptly executed.

In my wanderings about Cedarville during that day, I noticed a small but very neat cottage, a little way from the centre of the village. There was not around it a great profusion of flowers and shrubbery; but the few vines, flowers, and bushes that grew green and flourishing about the door, and along the clean walks, added to the air of taste and comfort that so peculiarly marked the dwelling.

"Who lives in that pleasant little spot?" I asked of a man whom I had frequently seen in Slade's bar-room. He happened to be passing the house at the same time that I was.

"Joe Morgan," was answered.

"Indeed!" I spoke in some surprise. "And what of Morgan? How is he doing?"

"Very well."

"Doesn't he drink?"

"No. Since the death of his child, he has never taken a drop. That event sobered him, and he has remained sober ever since."

"What is he doing?"

"Working at his old trade."

"That of a miller?"

"Yes. After Judge Hammond broke down, the distillery apparatus and cotton spinning machinery were all sold and removed from Cedarville. The purchaser of what remained, having something of the fear of God, as well as regard for man, in his heart, set himself to the restoration of the old order of things, and in due time the revolving mill-wheel was at its old and better work of grinding corn and wheat for bread. The only two men in Cedarville competent to take charge of the mill were Simon Slade and Joe Morgan. The first could not be had, and the second came in as a matter of course."

"And he remains sober and industrious?"

"As any man in the village," was the answer.

I saw but little of Slade or his son during the day. But both were in the bar-room at night, and both in a condition sorrowful to look upon. Their presence, together, in the bar-room, half intoxicated as they were, seemed to revive the unhappy temper of the previous evening, as freshly as if the sun had not risen and set upon their anger.

During the early part of the evening, considerable company was present, though not of a very select class. A large proportion were young men. To most of them the fact that Slade had fallen into the sheriff's hands was known; and I gathered from some aside conversation which reached my ears, that Frank's idle, spendthrift habits had hastened the present crisis in his father's affairs. He, too, was in debt to Judge Lyman—on what account, it was not hard to infer.

It was after nine o'clock, and there were not half a dozen persons in the room, when I noticed Frank Slade go behind the bar for the third or fourth time. He was just lifting a decanter of brandy, when his father, who was considerably under the influence of drink, started forward, and laid his hand upon that of his son. Instantly a fierce light gleamed from the eyes of the young man.

"Let go of my hand!" he exclaimed.

"No, I won't. Put up that brandy bottle—you're drunk now."

"Don't meddle with me, old man!" angrily retorted Frank. "I'm not in the mood to bear any thing more from *you*."

"You're drunk as a fool now," returned Slade, who had seized the decanter. "Let go the bottle."

For only an instant did the young man hesitate. Then he drove his half-clenched hand against the breast of his father, who went staggering away several paces from the counter. Recovering himself, and now almost furious, the landlord rushed forward upon his son, his hand raised to strike him.

"Keep off!" cried Frank. "Keep off! If you touch me, I'll strike you down!" At the same time raising the half-filled bottle threateningly.

But his father was in too maddened a state to fear any consequences, and so pressed forward upon his son, striking him in the face the moment he came near enough to do so.

Instantly, the young man, infuriated by drink and evil passions, threw the bottle at his father's head. The dangerous missile fell, crashing upon one of his temples, shivering it into a hundred pieces. A heavy, jarring fall too surely marked the fearful consequences of the blow. When we gathered around the fallen man, and made an effort to lift him from the floor, a thrill of horror went through every heart. A mortal paleness was already on his marred face, and the death-gurgle in his throat! In three minutes from the time the blow was struck, his spirit had gone upward to give an account of the deeds done in the body.

"Frank Slade! you have murdered your father!"

Sternly were these terrible words uttered. It was some time before the young man seemed to comprehend their meaning. But the moment he realized the awful truth, he uttered an exclamation of horror. Almost at the same instant, a pistol-shot came sharply on the ear. But the meditated self-destruction was not accomplished. The aim was not surely taken; and the ball struck harmlessly against the ceiling.

Half an hour afterward, and Frank Slade was a lonely prisoner in the county jail!

Does the reader need a word of comment on this fearful consummation? No: and we will offer none.

"Frank Slade! You have murdered your Father!"

NIGHT THE TENTH.

THE CLOSING SCENE AT THE "SICKLE AND SHEAF."

ON the day that succeeded the evening of this fearful tragedy, placards were to be seen all over the village, announcing a mass meeting at the "Sickle and Sheaf" that night.

By early twilight, the people commenced assembling. The bar, which had been closed all day, was now thrown open, and lighted; and in this room, where so much of evil had been originated, encouraged, and consummated, a crowd of earnest-looking men were soon gathered. Among them I saw the fine person of Mr. Hargrove. Joe Morgan—or rather, Mr. Morgan—was also of the number. The latter I would scarcely have recognized, had not some one near me called him by name. He was well dressed, stood erect, and though there

were many deep lines on his thoughtful countenance, all traces of his former habits were
gone. While I was observing him, he arose,
and addressing a few words to the assemblage,
nominated Mr. Hargrove as chairman of the
meeting. To this a unanimous assent was
given.

On taking the chair, Mr. Hargrove made a
brief address, something to this effect.

"Ten years ago," said he, his voice evincing
a slight unsteadiness as he began, but growing
firmer as he proceeded, "there was not a happier spot in Bolton county than Cedarville.
Now, the marks of ruin are everywhere. Ten
years ago, there was a kind-hearted, industrious
miller in Cedarville, liked by every one, and as
harmless as a little child. Now, his bloated,
disfigured body lies in that room. His death
was violent, and by the hand of his own
son!"

Mr. Hargrove's words fell slowly, distinctly,
and marked by the most forcible emphasis.

There was scarcely one present who did not feel a low shudder run along his nerves, as the last words were spoken in a husky whisper.

"Ten years ago," he proceeded, "the miller had a happy wife, and two innocent, glad-hearted children. Now, his wife, bereft of reason, is in a mad-house, and his son the occupant of a felon's cell, charged with the awful crime of parricide!"

Briefly he paused, while his audience stood gazing upon him with half-suspended respiration.

"Ten years ago," he went on, "Judge Hammond was accounted the richest man in Cedarville. Yesterday he was carried, a friendless pauper, to the Alms-house; and to-day he is the unmourned occupant of a pauper's grave! Ten years ago, his wife was the proud, hopeful, loving mother of a most promising son. I need not describe what Willy Hammond was. All here knew him well. Ah! what shattered the fine intellect of that noble-minded woman?

Why did her heart break? Where is she? Where is Willy Hammond?"

A low, half-repressed groan answered the speaker.

"Ten years ago, you, sir," pointing to a sad-looking old man, and calling him by name, "had two sons—generous, promising, manly-hearted boys. What are they now? You need not answer the question. Too well is their history and your sorrow known. Ten years ago, I had a son,—amiable, kind, loving, but weak. Heaven knows how I sought to guard and protect him! But he fell also. The arrows of destruction darkened the very air of our once secure and happy village. And who was safe? Not mine, nor yours!

"Shall I go on? Shall I call up and pass in review before you, one after another, all the wretched victims who have fallen in Cedarville during the last ten years? Time does not permit. It would take hours for the enumeration! No; I will not throw additional darkness into the picture. Heaven knows it is black enough already! But what is the root of this great evil? Where lies the fearful secret? Who understands the disease? A direful pestilence is in the air—it walketh in darkness, and wasteth at noonday. It is slaying the first-born in our houses, and the cry of anguish is swelling on every gale. Is there no remedy?"

"Yes! yes! There is a remedy!" was the spontaneous answer from many voices.

"Be it our task, then, to find and apply it this night," answered the chairman, as he took his seat.

"And there is but one remedy," said Morgan, as Mr. Hargrove sat down. "The accursed traffic must cease among us. You must cut off the fountain, if you would dry up the stream. If you would save the young, the weak, and the innocent—on you God has laid the solemn duty of their protection—you must cover them from the tempter. Evil is strong, wily, fierce, and active in the pursuit of its ends. The

young, the weak, and the innocent can no more
resist its assaults, than the lamb can resist the
wolf.   They are helpless, if you abandon them
to the powers of evil.   Men and brethren! as
one who has himself been well-nigh lost—as
one who, daily, feels and trembles at the dangers that beset his path—I do conjure you to
stay the fiery stream that is bearing every thing
good and beautiful among you to destruction.
Fathers! for the sake of your young children,
be up now and doing.   Think of Willy Hammond, Frank Slade, and a dozen more whose
names I could repeat, and hesitate no longer!
Let us resolve, this night, that from henceforth
the traffic shall cease in Cedarville.   Is there
not a large majority of citizens in favor of such
a measure?   And whose rights or interests can
be affected by such a restriction?   Who, in
fact, has any right to sow disease and death in
our community?   The liberty, under suffer-
ance, to do so, wrongs the individual who uses
it, as well as those who become his victims.

Do you want proof of this? Look at Simon Slade, the happy, kind-hearted miller; and at Simon Slade, the tavern-keeper. Was he benefited by the liberty to work harm to his neighbor? No! no! In heaven's name, then, let the traffic cease! To this end, I offer these resolutions:—

"Be it resolved by the inhabitants of Cedarville, That from this day henceforth, no more intoxicating drink shall be sold within the limits of the corporation.

"Resolved, further, That all the liquors in the 'Sickle and Sheaf' be forthwith destroyed, and that a fund be raised to pay the creditors of Simon Slade therefor, should they demand compensation.

"Resolved, That in closing up all other places where liquor is sold, regard shall be had to the right of property which the law secures to every man.

"Resolved, That with the consent of the legal authorities, all the liquor for sale in Cedar ville be destroyed, provided the owners thereof be paid its full value out of a fund specially raised for that purpose."

But for the calm yet resolute opposition of one or two men, these resolutions would have passed by acclamation. A little sober argument showed the excited company that no good end is ever secured by the adoption of wrong means.

There were, in Cedarville, regularly constituted authorities, which alone had the power to determine public measures, or to say what business might or might not be pursued by individuals. And through these authorities they must act in an orderly way.

There was some little chafing at this view of the case. But good sense and reason prevailed. Somewhat modified, the resolutions passed, and the more ultra-inclined contented themselves with carrying out the second resolution, to destroy forthwith all the liquor to be found on the premises; which was immediately done.

After which the people dispersed to their homes, each with a lighter heart, and better hopes for the future of their village.

On the next day, as I entered the stage that was to bear me from Cedarville, I saw a man strike his sharp axe into the worn, faded, and leaning post that had, for so many years, borne aloft the "Sickle and Sheaf;" and, just as the driver gave word to his horses, the false emblem which had invited so many to enter the way of destruction, fell crashing to the earth.

THE END.

The Two Babylons
Alexander Hislop

You may be surprised to learn that many traditions of Roman Catholicism in fact don't come from Christ's teachings but from an ancient Babylonian "Mystery" religion that was centered on Nimrod, his wife Semiramis, and a child Tammuz. This book shows how this ancient religion transformed itself as it incorporated Christ into its teachings....

Religion/History   Pages:358

ISBN: *1-59462-010-5*   MSRP *$22.95*   QTY

The Power Of Concentration
Theron Q. Dumont

It is of the utmost value to learn how to concentrate. To make the greatest success of anything you must be able to concentrate your entire thought upon the idea you are working on. The person that is able to concentrate utilizes all constructive thoughts and shuts out all destructive ones...

Self Help/Inspirational   Pages:196

ISBN: *1-59462-141-1*   MSRP *$14.95*

Rightly Dividing The Word
Clarence Larkin

The "Fundamental Doctrines" of the Christian Faith are clearly outlined in numerous books on Theology, but they are not available to the average reader and were mainly written for students. The Author has made it the work of his ministry to preach the "Fundamental Doctrines." To this end he has aimed to express them in the simplest and clearest manner..

Religion   Pages:352

ISBN: *1-59462-334-1*   MSRP *$23.45*

The Law of Psychic Phenomena
Thomson Jay Hudson

"I do not expect this book to stand upon its literary merits; for if it is unsound in principle, felicity of diction cannot save it, and if sound, homeliness of expression cannot destroy it. My primary object in offering it to the public is to assist in bringing Psychology within the domain of the exact sciences. That this has never been accomplished..."

New Age   Pages:420

ISBN: *1-59462-124-1*   MSRP *$29.95*

Beautiful Joe
Marshall Saunders

When Marshall visited the Moore family in 1892, she discovered Joe, a dog they had nursed back to health from his previous abusive home to live a happy life. So moved was she, that she wrote this classic masterpiece which won accolades and was recognized as a heartwarming symbol for humane animal treatment...

Fiction   Pages:256

ISBN: *1-59462-261-2*   MSRP *$18.45*

The Codes Of Hammurabi And
Moses - W. W. Davies

The discovery of the Hammurabi Code is one of the greatest achievements of archaeology, and is of paramount interest, not only to the student of the Bible, but also to all those interested in ancient history...

Religion   Pages:132

ISBN: *1-59462-338-4*   MSRP *$12.95*

The Thirty-Six Dramatic Situations
Georges Polti

An incredibly useful guide for aspiring authors and playwrights. This volume categorizes every dramatic situation which could occur in a story and describes them in a list of 36 situations. A great aid to help inspire or formalize the creative writing process...

Self Help/Reference   Pages:204

ISBN: *1-59462-134-9*   MSRP *$15.95*

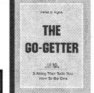

The Go-Getter
Kyne B. Peter

The Go Getter is the story of William Peck.He was a war veteran and amputee who will not be refused what he wants. Peck not only fights to find employment but continually proves himself more than competent at the many difficult test that are throw his way in the course of his early days with the Ricks Lumber Company...

Business/Self Help/Inspirational   Pages:68

ISBN: *1-59462-186-1*   MSRP *$8.95*   QTY

Self Mastery
Emile Coue

Emile Coue came up with novel way to improve the lives of people. He was a pharmacist by trade and often saw ailing people. This lead him to develop autosuggestion, a form of self-hypnosis. At the time his theories weren't popular but over the years evidence is mounting that he was indeed right all along...

New Age/Self Help   Pages:98

ISBN: *1-59462-189-6*   MSRP *$7.95*

The Awful Disclosures Of
Maria Monk

"I cannot banish the scenes and characters of this book from my memory. To me it can never appear like an amusing fable, or lose its interest and importance. The story is one which is continually before me, and must return fresh to my mind with painful emotions as long as I live..."

Religion   Pages:232

ISBN: *1-59462-160-8*   MSRP *$17.95*

As a Man Thinketh
James Allen

"This little volume (the result of meditation and experience) is not intended as an exhaustive treatise on the much-written-upon subject of the power of thought. It is suggestive rather than explanatory, its object being to stimulate men and women to the discovery and perception of the truth that by virtue of the thoughts which they choose and encourage..."

Inspirational/Self Help   Pages:80

ISBN: *1-59462-231-0*   MSRP *$9.45*

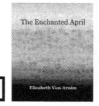

The Enchanted April
Elizabeth Von Arnim

It began in a woman's club in London on a February afternoon, an uncomfortable club, and a miserable afternoon when Mrs. Wilkins, who had come down from Hampstead to shop and had lunched at her club, took up The Times from the table in the smoking-room...

Fiction   Pages:368

ISBN: *1-59462-150-0*   MSRP *$23.45*

Holland - The History Of Netherlands
Thomas Colley Grattan

Thomas Grattan was a prestigious writer from Dublin who served as British Consul to the US. Among his works is an authoritative look at the history of Holland. A colorful and interesting look at history....

History/Politics   Pages:408

ISBN: *1-59462-137-3*   MSRP *$26.95*

A Concise Dictionary of Middle English
A. L. Mayhew
Walter W. Skeat

The present work is intended to meet, in some measure, the requirements of those who wish to make some study of Middle-English, and who find a difficulty in obtaining such assistance as will enable them to find out the meanings and etymologies of the words most essential to their purpose...

Reference/History   Pages:332

ISBN: *1-59462-119-5*   MSRP *$29.95*

BOOK JUNGLE

Bringing Classics to Life

www.bookjungle.com *email: sales@bookjungle.com fax: 630-214-0564 mail: Book Jungle PO Box 2226 Champaign, IL 61825*

The Witch-Cult in Western Europe
Margaret Murray

QTY

The mass of existing material on this subject is so great that I have not attempted to make a survey of the whole of European 'Witchcraft' but have confined myself to an intensive study of the cult in Great Britain. In order, however, to obtain a clearer understanding of the ritual and beliefs I have had recourse to French and Flemish sources...

Occult **Pages:308**
ISBN: *1-59462-126-8* MSRP *$22.45*

Philosophy Of Natural Therapeutics
Henry Lindlahr

QTY

We invite the earnest cooperation in this great work of all those who have awakened to the necessity for more rational living and for radical reform in healing methods...

Health/Philosophy/Self Help **Pages:552**
ISBN: *1-59462-132-2* MSRP *$34.95*

The Science Of Psychic Healing
Yogi Ramacharaka

This book is not a book of theories it deals with facts. Its author regards the best of theories as but working hypotheses to be used only until better ones present themselves. The "fact" is the principal thing the essential thing to uncover which the tool, theory, is used...

New Age/Health **Pages:180**
ISBN: *1-59462-140-3* MSRP *$13.95*

A Message to Garcia
Elbert Hubbard

This literary trifle, A Message to Garcia, was written one evening after supper, in a single hour. It was on the Twenty-second of February, Eighteen Hundred Ninety-nine, Washington's Birthday, and we were just going to press with the March Philistine...

New Age/Fiction **Pages:92**
ISBN: *1-59462-144-6* MSRP *$9.95*

Bible Myths
Thomas Doane

In pursuing the study of the Bible Myths, facts pertaining thereto, in a condensed form, seemed to be greatly needed, and nowhere to be found. Widely scattered through hundreds of ancient and modern volumes, most of the contents of this book may indeed be found; but any previous attempt to trace exclusively the myths and legends...

Religion/History **Pages:644**
ISBN: *1-59462-163-2* MSRP *$38.95*

The Book of Jasher
Alcuinus Flaccus Albinus

The Book of Jasher is an historical religious volume that many consider as a missing holy book from the Old Testament. Particularly studied by the Church of Later Day Saints and historians, it covers the history of the world from creation until the period of Judges in Israel. It's authenticity is bolstered due to a reference to the Book of Jasher in the Bible in Joshua 10:13

Religion/History **Pages:276**
ISBN: *1-59462-197-7* MSRP *$18.95*

Tertium Organum
P. D. Ouspensky

A truly mind expanding writing that combines science with mysticism with unprecedented elegance. He presents the world we live in as a multi dimensional world and time as a motion through this world. But this isn't a cold and purely analytical explanation but a masterful presentation filled with similes and analogies...

New Age **Pages:356**
ISBN: *1-59462-205-1* MSRP *$23.95*

The Titan
Theodore Dreiser

"When Frank Algernon Cowperwood emerged from the Eastern District Penitentiary, in Philadelphia he realized that the old life he had lived in that city since boyhood was ended. His youth was gone, and with it had been lost the great business prospects of his earlier manhood. He must begin again..."

Fiction **Pages:564**
ISBN: *1-59462-220-5* MSRP *$33.95*

Advance Course in Yogi Philosophy
Yogi Ramacharaka

"The twelve lessons forming this volume were originally issued in the shape of monthly lessons, known as "The Advanced Course in Yogi Philosophy and Oriental Occultism" during a period of twelve months beginning with October, 1904, and ending September, 1905."

Philosophy/Inspirational/Self Help **Pages:340**
ISBN: *1-59462-229-9* MSRP *$22.95*

Biblical Essays
J. B. Lightfoot

About one-third of the present volume has already seen the light. The opening essay "On the Internal Evidence for the Authenticity and Genuineness of St John's Gospel" was published in the "Expositor" in the early months of 1890, and has been reprinted since...

Religion/History **Pages:480**
ISBN: *1-59462-238-8* MSRP *$30.95*

Ambassador Morgenthau's Story
Henry Morgenthau

"By this time the American people have probably become convinced that the Germans deliberately planned the conquest of the world. Yet they hesitate to convict on circumstantial evidence and for this reason all eye witnesses to this, the greatest crime in modern history, should volunteer their testimony..."

History **Pages:472**
ISBN: *1-59462-244-2* MSRP *$29.95*

The Settlement Cook Book
Simon Kander

A legacy from the civil war, this book is a classic "American charity cookbook," which was used for fundraisers starting in Milwaukee. While it has transformed over the years, this printing provides great recipes from American history. Over two million copies have been sold. This volume contains a rich collection of recipes from noted chefs and hostesses of the turn of the century...

How-to **Pages:472**
ISBN: *1-59462-256-6* MSRP *$29.95*

The Aquarian Gospel of Jesus the Christ
Levi Dowling

A retelling of Jesus' story which tells us what happened during the twenty year gap left by the Bible's New Testament. It tells of his travels to the far-east where he studied with the masters and fought against the rigid caste system. This book has enjoyed a resurgence in modern America and provides spiritual insight with charm. Its influences can be seen throughout the Age of Aquarius.

Religion **Pages:264**
ISBN: *1-59462-321-X* MSRP *$18.95*

My Life and Work
Henry Ford

Henry Ford revolutionized the world with his implementation of mass production for the Model T automobile. Gain valuable business insight into his life and work with his own auto-biography... "We have only started on our development of our country we have not as yet, with all our talk of wonderful progress, done more than scratch the surface. The progress has been wonderful enough but..."

Biographies/History/Business **Pages:300**
ISBN: *1-59462-198-5* MSRP *$21.95*

QTY

☐	**The Rosicrucian Cosmo-Conception Mystic Christianity** *by Max Heindel* ISBN: *1-59462-188-8* **$38.95** *The Rosicrucian Cosmo-conception is not dogmatic, neither does it appeal to any other authority than the reason of the student. It is: not controversial, but is: sent forth in the, hope that it may help to clear..* New Age/Religion Pages 646
☐	**Abandonment To Divine Providence** *by Jean-Pierre de Caussade* ISBN: *1-59462-228-0* **$25.95** *"The Rev. Jean Pierre de Caussade was one of the most remarkable spiritual writers of the Society of Jesus in France in the 18th Century. His death took place at Toulouse in 1751. His works have gone through many editions and have been republished...* Inspirational/Religion Pages 400
☐	**Mental Chemistry** *by Charles Haanel* ISBN: *1-59462-192-6* **$23.95** *Mental Chemistry allows the change of material conditions by combining and appropriately utilizing the power of the mind. Much like applied chemistry creates something new and unique out of careful combinations of chemicals the mastery of mental chemistry...* New Age Pages 354
☐	**The Letters of Robert Browning and Elizabeth Barret Barrett 1845-1846 vol II** ISBN: *1-59462-193-4* **$35.95** *by Robert Browning and Elizabeth Barrett* Biographies Pages 596
☐	**Gleanings In Genesis (volume I)** *by Arthur W. Pink* ISBN: *1-59462-130-6* **$27.45** *Appropriately has Genesis been termed "the seed plot of the Bible" for in it we have, in germ form, almost all of the great doctrines which are afterwards fully developed in the books of Scripture which follow...* Religion/Inspirational Pages 420
☐	**The Master Key** *by L. W. de Laurence* ISBN: *1-59462-001-6* **$30.95** *In no branch of human knowledge has there been a more lively increase of the spirit of research during the past few years than in the study of Psychology, Concentration and Mental Discipline. The requests for authentic lessons in Thought Control, Mental Discipline and...* New Age/Business Pages 422
☐	**The Lesser Key Of Solomon Goetia** *by L. W. de Laurence* ISBN: *1-59462-092-X* **$9.95** *This translation of the first book of the "Lemegton" which is now for the first time made accessible to students of Talismanic Magic was done, after careful collation and edition, from numerous Ancient Manuscripts in Hebrew, Latin, and French...* New Age/Occult Pages 92
☐	**Rubaiyat Of Omar Khayyam** *by Edward Fitzgerald* ISBN:*1-59462-332-5* **$13.95** *Edward Fitzgerald, whom the world has already learned, in spite of his own efforts to remain within the shadow of anonymity, to look upon as one of the rarest poets of the century, was born at Bredfield, in Suffolk, on the 31st of March, 1809. He was the third son of John Purcell...* Music Pages 172
☐	**Ancient Law** *by Henry Maine* ISBN: *1-59462-128-4* **$29.95** *The chief object of the following pages is to indicate some of the earliest ideas of mankind, as they are reflected in Ancient Law, and to point out the relation of those ideas to modern thought.* Religion/History Pages 452
☐	**Far-Away Stories** *by William J. Locke* ISBN: *1-59462-129-2* **$19.45** *"Good wine needs no bush, but a collection of mixed vintages does. And this book is just such a collection. Some of the stories I do not want to remain buried for ever in the museum files of dead magazine-numbers an author's not unpardonable vanity..."* Fiction Pages 272
☐	**Life of David Crockett** *by David Crockett* ISBN: *1-59462-250-7* **$27.45** *"Colonel David Crockett was one of the most remarkable men of the times in which he lived. Born in humble life, but gifted with a strong will, an indomitable courage, and unremitting perseverance..* Biographies/New Age Pages 424
☐	**Lip-Reading** *by Edward Nitchie* ISBN: *1-59462-206-X* **$25.95** *Edward B. Nitchie, founder of the New York School for the Hard of Hearing, now the Nitchie School of Lip-Reading, Inc, wrote "LIP-READING Principles and Practice". The development and perfecting of this meritorious work on lip-reading was an undertaking...* How-to Pages 400
☐	**A Handbook of Suggestive Therapeutics, Applied Hypnotism, Psychic Science** ISBN: *1-59462-214-0* **$24.95** *by Henry Munro* Health New Age/Health/Self-help Pages 376
☐	**A Doll's House: and Two Other Plays** *by Henrik Ibsen* ISBN: *1-59462-112-8* **$19.95** *Henrik Ibsen created this classic when in revolutionary 1848 Rome. Introducing some striking concepts in playwriting for the realist genre, this play has been studied the world over.* Fiction/Classics/Plays 308
☐	**The Light of Asia** *by sir Edwin Arnold* ISBN: *1-59462-204-3* **$13.95** *In this poetic masterpiece, Edwin Arnold describes the life and teachings of Buddha. The man who was to become known as Buddha to the world was born as Prince Gautama of India but he rejected the worldly riches and abandoned the reigns of power when... Religion/History/Biographies Pages 170*
☐	**The Complete Works of Guy de Maupassant** *by Guy de Maupassant* ISBN: *1-59462-157-8* **$16.95** *"For days and days, nights and nights, I had dreamed of that first kiss which was to consecrate our engagement, and I knew not on what spot I should put my lips..."* Fiction/Classics Pages 240
☐	**The Art of Cross-Examination** *by Francis L. Wellman* ISBN: *1-59462-309-0* **$26.95** *Written by a renowned trial lawyer, Wellman imparts his experience and uses case studies to explain how to use psychology to extract desired information through questioning.* How-to/Science/Reference Pages 408
☐	**Answered or Unanswered?** *by Louisa Vaughan* ISBN: *1-59462-248-5* **$10.95** *Miracles of Faith in China* Religion Pages 112
☐	**The Edinburgh Lectures on Mental Science (1909)** *by Thomas* ISBN: *1-59462-008-3* **$11.95** *This book contains the substance of a course of lectures recently given by the writer in the Queen Street Hall, Edinburgh. Its purpose is to indicate the Natural Principles governing the relation between Mental Action and Material Conditions...* New Age/Psychology Pages 148
☐	**Ayesha** *by H. Rider Haggard* ISBN: *1-59462-301-5* **$24.95** *Verily and indeed it is the unexpected that happens! Probably if there was one person upon the earth from whom the Editor of this, and of a certain previous history, did not expect to hear again...* Classics Pages 380
☐	**Ayala's Angel** *by Anthony Trollope* ISBN: *1-59462-352-X* **$29.95** *The two girls were both pretty, but Lucy who was twenty-one who supposed to be simple and comparatively unattractive, whereas Ayala was credited, as her Bombwhat romantic name might show, with poetic charm and a taste for romance. Ayala when her father died was nineteen...* Fiction Pages 484
☐	**The American Commonwealth** *by James Bryce* ISBN: *1-59462-286-8* **$34.45** *An interpretation of American democratic political theory. It examines political mechanics and society from the perspective of Scotsman James Bryce* Politics Pages 572
☐	**Stories of the Pilgrims** *by Margaret P. Pumphrey* ISBN: *1-59462-116-0* **$17.95** *This book explores pilgrims religious oppression in England as well as their escape to Holland and eventual crossing to America on the Mayflower, and their early days in New England...* History Pages 268

QTY

The Fasting Cure *by Sinclair Upton*   ISBN: *1-59462-222-1*   **$13.95**
In the Cosmopolitan Magazine for May, 1910, and in the Contemporary Review (London) for April, 1910, I published an article dealing with my experiences in fasting. I have written a great many magazine articles, but never one which attracted so much attention... New Age/Self Help/Health Pages 164

Hebrew Astrology *by Sepharial*   ISBN: *1-59462-308-2*   **$13.45**
In these days of advanced thinking it is a matter of common observation that we have left many of the old landmarks behind and that we are now pressing forward to greater heights and to a wider horizon than that which represented the mind-content of our progenitors... Astrology Pages 144

Thought Vibration or The Law of Attraction in the Thought World   ISBN: *1-59462-127-6*   **$12.95**
by William Walker Atkinson   *Psychology/Religion Pages 144*

Optimism *by Helen Keller*   ISBN: *1-59462-108-X*   **$15.95**
Helen Keller was blind, deaf, and mute since 19 months old, yet famously learned how to overcome these handicaps, and spread her lectures promoting optimism. An inspiring read for everyone... Biographies/Inspirational Pages 84

Sara Crewe *by Frances Burnett*   ISBN: *1-59462-360-0*   **$9.45**
In the first place, Miss Minchin lived in London. Her home was a large, dull, tall one, in a large, dull square, where all the houses were alike, and all the sparrows were alike, and where all the door-knockers made the same heavy sound... Childrens Classic Pages 88

The Autobiography of Benjamin Franklin *by Benjamin Franklin*   ISBN: *1-59462-135-7*   **$24.95**
The Autobiography of Benjamin Franklin has probably been more extensively read than any other American historical work, and no other book of its kind has had such ups and downs of fortune. Franklin lived for many years in England, where he was agent... Biographies/History Pages 332

Name	
Email	
Telephone	
Address	
City, State ZIP	

☐ **Credit Card**   ☐ **Check / Money Order**

Credit Card Number	
Expiration Date	
Signature	

Please Mail to: Book Jungle
PO Box 2226
Champaign, IL 61825
or Fax to: 630-214-0564

ORDERING INFORMATION

web: *www.bookjungle.com*
email: *sales@bookjungle.com*
fax: *630-214-0564*
mail: *Book Jungle PO Box 2226 Champaign, IL 61825*
or PayPal *to sales@bookjungle.com*

DIRECT-ORDER TERMS

20% Discount if You Order Two or More Books
Free Domestic Shipping!
Accepted: Master Card, Visa, Discover, American Express

Please contact us for bulk discounts

CPSIA information can be obtained
at www.ICGtesting.com
Printed in the USA
LVHW101554261219
641750LV00006B/242/P